THE MIDNIGHT PRESS

AND

OTHER OXFORD STORIES

Thanks so much for
all your help and
support in 2015.
Pam Peirson

THE MIDNIGHT PRESS

AND

OTHER OXFORD STORIES

OxPens

www.oxpens.co.uk

First published in Great Britain 2013 by OxPens in conjunction with
WritersPrintShop

ISBN 9781780185422

Printed and bound in the UK by
PublishPoint from KnowledgePoint Limited,Reading

The cover image is by Valerie Petts and is reproduced by kind
permission of the artist.

Tim Kirtley drew the map of the Old Jewish Quarter of Oxford for
'Turn Right at Fish Street'

This novel is a work of fiction and the characters and events in it exist
only in its pages and in the authors' imagination

The profits from this book will be shared with Oxford Homeless
Pathways (formerly Oxford Night Shelter).

CONTENTS

FOREWORD

In my youthful years – now almost totally misremembered – I used to think that the *'Short Story'* genre was considerably more attractive to the majority of readers than the *'Full Novel'* variety. In addition, I thought I knew that the very simple, and very precise reason for such a preference, was that the former kind of writing was considerably shorter in length than the latter, and could be read through far more quickly. And so? So if I were getting rather bored with the first story chosen, I could easily abandon ship completely, and try the *'second shortest'* offering in the collected tales.

In my mid-teens, in a ragged sort of way, I enjoyed the works of Conan Doyle and G K Chesterton, although I was never quite so dazzled as the majority of my classmates by Sherlock Holmes and Father Brown. Perhaps it's just that crime has always fascinated me, although I remember in the 11+ examination it took me a mighty long while to answer the following: Rearrange the letters MERCI in order to make a word meaning 'an act that is against the law'. But however hard I try, I have never overmuch enjoyed any short story which is dependent for its dénouement on a supernatural or paranormal factor. No *deus ex machina* for me, thank you. So it is that I've always applauded a story which has a firm, unequivocal explanation of things. In fact I've always longed for surprise endings; and I once decided that if I had managed to spot the crook halfway through any text, I would not be over-inclined to try another work by the same author. Yes, I have often thought that Agatha Christie has twice as much imagination as the rest of us plotters and plodders put together!

But let me throw the curtain more widely open.

Not infrequently I am asked to recommend (if possible!) a batch of short stories for publication. And when (or if) I receive some acknowledgement from the potential publisher, I have become accustomed to being told that the short story is not the most popular genre in the reading habits of the great British public. In fact I learned recently from a well-known publisher that he could no longer consider short stories by any author who was not already an established name. Another purchase of string, stamps, and wrapping-paper for some possibly excellent scribblers. Yet there are, in my view, two isolated flickers of light visible on the bleak horizon.

But wait a minute! Let me briefly mention the obvious truth that there are a good many wonderfully able masters (and mistresses) of the genre to whom I have rarely paid appropriate appreciation. Who are they? In my lifetime, O Henry, Wodehouse, Saki... The first of this trio has been in my opinion the brightest, keenest short-story writer of anyone in the field, and his work has brought me greater sheer joy than any. Wait a while though! I reserve my first prize for Rudyard Kipling. What a genius that man was! And his greatest stories? Try *Love-o'-Women* and *On Greenhow Hill* – each of which is able to reduce the driest-eyed of readers to saddened tears.

And now what about those two beacons of promise I referred to earlier? First, it has pleased me enormously that a group of writers, some by now familiar names and some new voices have combined forces, for the fourth book in this series, to present to us another splendid arrangement of original Oxford short stories. An undoubted reason for the continued success of these ventures has been the talents of our individual contributors. By which I refer not only to the honing of their literary skills – spelling, punctuation, syntax, etc. – but also to their widened vision of the potential of the short story as a thriving component of English literature. And the second biggest factor in their success is that we have 'Oxford' on our side. Oxford is not only a beautiful word; it is also a beautiful city. And our writers manage, somehow, to winkle out each year some fascinating aspects of our city – its history, its buildings, its streets and its alleyways – a never-ending stream of anecdotes and linkages which we could never have guessed at. And, as one of our writers told me, 'Oxford as a place seems somehow able to push us ever higher and higher in our love and understanding of the city'. Would that I could have expressed my thoughts as well as that young lady. Here again then, (praise be!) we have further exemplification of that admirable sentiment.

Yet let me issue one vital caveat here: don't take too much notice of other people's criticism of your writing. I never had much adverse comment myself because I made use of the simple expedient of never letting anyone read my first draft except the publishers. But what if I received the following? 'After such a splendid Chapter One, I was hugely disappointed to find Chapter Two tedious and repetitive, with the plot advanced not even a millimetre after seven pages. I suggest a radical rewriting of this chapter; and I would be wholly glad if you would agree to omit it altogether.' What does one do then? Now, *if you agree*, shout 'Hallelujah', and accept the second suggestion. If you disagree? This is when you have to defend your corner, and insist, in biblical terms, 'What I have written, I have written!' I would myself call that 'artistic integrity'.

Finally, and specifically, can we all pay our heartfelt tribute to Linora and to Gina, both of whom have kept their watchful editorial eyes on the entries submitted for this present anthology by our loyal and talented lieutenants.

COLIN DEXTER

x

FANCY RUNNING INTO YOU

MARGARET PELLING

From the shelter of the shop doorway, Lucy Granger kept another doorway just up the High Street in her sights: the main doorway of the Examination Schools. Mike had to be coming out soon. His lecture on Roman imperialism finished at ten on Tuesday mornings. She looked at her watch again. It was five past.

Ah. There he was.

He began walking up the High Street, walking fast. She had to run, almost, to keep pace with him. She stayed about five yards behind him until the crossing, where she shrank back into another doorway until the green man flashed up and Mike started to cross. She quickly followed. She had to time this just right…

As he was turning in at the gate of Coventry College, she stepped forward. 'Oh, hello Mike, fancy running into you!'

He frowned. Then his eyes widened. '*Lucy?* Jesus Christ, what are you doing back in Oxford?'

'I'm working at St Matthew's. I'm a part time college office dogsbody, eleven till three. Oh, Mike, isn't this lovely? What do you say to a drink at the King's Arms later?'

'A drink? For God's sake, Lucy – look, come inside for a moment.'

He was inviting her into his college. He was actually taking her arm. Oh, joy! He stopped just inside the main gate. 'Now look, Lucy,' he said, leaning towards her, 'you were told not to keep following me.'

'It was an awfully long time ago, Mike. Five years three months and two days.'

'The court didn't mean just for five years, they meant you were never to come near me again, don't you understand?'

'I understand many things, Mike. I have a degree from this university. You were one of my tutors.'

'All right. So don't start all that again, OK? I'm going to my room now, and I'm never going to set eyes on you again. It's finished, Lucy.'

He walked away, but she didn't move. She stood there watching him cross the quad. It wasn't finished. In time, he would come to accept that. She just had to be patient, that was all.

The next thing was to see if he still lived in the house in Jericho, that house she'd been to that night... He might have moved. But he might not.

It was good that she and Mickey were living in Jericho too. Finding a flat to rent about five minutes' walk from that house: what a stroke of luck...

It was coming on to rain again. As she went through the main gate of St Matthew's and out into the street, Lucy pulled her jacket collar up. It wasn't much protection against the rain, but it was all she had. One of these days she'd remember to bring an umbrella. When she had less on her mind. When Mike had come to accept that it wasn't finished. She looked at her watch. Was there time to go into Sainsbury's before she picked up Mickey from school?

There wasn't time, not really. Which was why she was ten minutes late, and Mickey was standing in the playground with that spotty classroom assistant. But if she hadn't stopped to buy things for supper she'd have had to take him into the Co-op, and he'd have wanted treats which she couldn't afford on a college secretarial assistant's pay.

One of these days she'd stock the fridge in advance. When she had less on her mind.

'Sorry,' she said to the classroom assistant as she grabbed Mickey's hand. 'Lot on at work.'

'Can you *try* and be on time tomorrow, Ms Granger?' said the assistant, sighing.

'I will. It's just that...' Oh, never mind.

As they left the playground, Mickey started to whine and drag his feet. 'I getting *wet,*' he said.

'I know, sweetie, but if you walk fast we'll be home sooner. And Daddy's on TV tonight.'

'Don't *want* to watch Daddy on TV. Want to watch *Thomas the Tank Engine.*'

'Oh, but we must watch Daddy, darling. You'll be meeting him soon.'

After supper, Lucy settled Mickey down on the sofa with his mug of orange juice and put the DVD into the player. She sank back on the sofa with her coffee and put an arm around Mickey as *History Watch* began. A man came into view: 'This week we're going to hear from

2

Professor Michael Wadebridge of the University of Oxford,' said the man. She held her breath as the focus shifted to Mike, then let out a sigh. Ah *yes*. This was the best moment of the day.

'Say, "Hello Daddy",' she said to Mickey.

'Don't want to,' said Mickey.

'Oh, go on. Mummy will love you a lot if you do.'

Mickey sighed. 'HELLO DADDEE,' he shouted at the screen.

Lucy took a sip of coffee as she gazed at the tall, dark pony-tailed man in jeans and sunglasses who was standing on the battlement of an old fort with the sea behind. He would always be the man for her, the one and only. She pulled her feet up under her on the old sofa whose arms were leaking stuffing and let the sight of him fill her eyes. Everything here had seen better days, including the house this flat was in. Everything, that is, except the flat-screen TV that brought Mike to her every night without fail.

'...and down there are the Straits of Actium,' he was saying as the shot panned away from him to a Greek coastline. 'What happened down there in 31 BC changed world history. Picture the scene: Antony's ships are ranged all across the mouth of the gulf over there. Cleopatra's ships are some way behind – she isn't going to mix it with any Romans if she can help it. Wise? Out for what she can get? Take your pick, we don't know. Octavian's fleet is to seaward, blockading Antony, waiting to see what he'll do. It's a quiet sort of morning, but that's going to change...'

He was so good at this. She could listen to him for ever. And she would. She *would*.

When the episode ended, she let Mickey have his *Thomas the Tank Engine* DVD for a few minutes while she washed the supper dishes in the ancient sink with the dripping taps. This was the worst moment of the day. Another twenty four hours to get through before she played her DVD again. Unless she played it after Mickey was in bed... Why hadn't she thought of that before? She could play it over and over...

Susan Wadebridge saw the woman through the living room window. Again? That was the third time this week.

She waited until Amy and Ruth were in bed and she and Mike were sitting down to supper: 'Mike,' she said as he poured glasses of wine for them, 'I thought I knew everybody in this neighbourhood, but there's a new woman around. I see her going up the street every afternoon at half past three with a boy of about five in tow.'

He looked at her, frowning. 'She'll have just collected her kid

3

from school, that's why she's always there at the same time,' he said.

'Mm. Probably. She seems to be very interested in this house, though...' She shrugged. 'Maybe I watch too many TV cop shows.'

Mike grinned. But he was a bit quiet for the rest of supper, she noticed. And he went to the study after they'd cleared up, saying he was behind with preparing tomorrow's lecture.

Old girlfriends from Mike's very sociable past did pop up from time to time. But this would be the first who had a child.

The next afternoon, Susan was in the Co-op in Walton Street. Who should be two places ahead of her in the queue but the woman? No boy this time, but school wasn't out yet. The woman paid and left. The man in front was buying only cigarettes, and Susan was buying only milk and bread, and so it happened that the woman was still within sight when Susan came out of the shop.

A woman on her own can normally walk faster than a woman with one child in a buggy and another on reins, but not the one ahead of Susan. From behind, there was something almost pathetic about her: the way she was dragging her feet, for a start. She had straggly mousey-brown hair, and the coat hanging from her thin shoulders looked like an Oxfam reject. Single parent, lonely, probably not much money... It wasn't hard to sum her up. School was just coming out, but the woman kept on going until she reached one of the streets down by the canal. Susan watched her let herself into a house about half way along. Maybe the boy wasn't at school today. He might be ill, and the woman had nipped out while he was asleep or watching TV.

Susan walked past the house. She noted the number.

The following afternoon, the woman appeared outside the Wadebridges' house. This time the boy was with her. Susan made a decision. She slipped outside, grabbed the food waste bin from its alcove by the door – lucky that it was bin day tomorrow – and headed down the garden path.

'Oh hello,' she said. 'I've often seen you passing recently. Are you new in the neighbourhood?' She gave the woman her brightest smile, but had to stop herself recoiling as she found herself looking into a face that was deathly white. The eyes were big dark pools. The woman must once have been beautiful. Now, she just looked wasted. Wasted – and terrified.

'I – I...' began the woman, but looking more at Amy, in Susan's arms, than at Susan herself. The boy was kicking at a piece of gravel on the pavement and pulling the woman's hand. There was a sad, bedraggled air about him, poor scrap. Something in her wanted to give him a hug.

'She's teething,' said Susan, indicating Amy. 'She's having one of her clingy days.'

There came a voice from behind: 'Mummy, want to do a wee!' Susan looked back to see Ruth standing in the doorway, fidgeting from foot to foot.

'I'd better go,' said Susan, pumping up her smile. All the way back up the path, her neck was prickling. She'd bet the woman was just standing there, watching her.

That evening at supper she said to Mike, 'I saw that woman again today.'

It seemed to her that he paused for a second or so before saying, 'Woman? What woman?'

'You know, the one I keep seeing going past the house. Only today, I talked to her.'

He put his fork down and stared at her. 'You did? What did she say?'

Not *what did you say*, but *what did she say*. Interesting.

'Oh, nothing much. We just passed the time of day. I know where she lives, though.' She told him, but didn't mention how she knew. Let him think the address had fallen casually into the conversation.

Mike was quiet again for the rest of the meal. Afterwards he went to his study saying he had a pile of papers to get through for a committee meeting tomorrow. He didn't emerge until she was brushing her teeth before bed. She heard him going downstairs:

'Just popping out for a quick stroll around the block to clear my head,' he called.

'Fine,' she called back.

When the front door had closed, she took a deep, slow breath. 'Fine,' she repeated, in a murmur. *Right.* She put her head into the girls' room – both were fast asleep – then threw on jeans and a jacket over her pyjamas.

She followed Mike through the streets of Jericho. She watched him go up to the woman's house and ring the bell. A moment or so later, he went in. She turned in the direction of home, her heart beating fast.

'Mike! It's you!' Lucy's heart lifted. That moment this afternoon of seeing the woman, the children, the horror of it – was it all a nightmare, was she about to wake? 'How did you find me?'

'Never mind that. Can I come in?'

'Of course, of course!' She led him up the narrow stairs, calling, 'Mickey, Mickey, wake up, it's Daddy!'

'Lucy –' Mike began, but she couldn't stop, not when he had to see his son, simply *had* to. She ran into the bedroom and scooped up the still-sleeping Mickey. As she carried him into the living room he woke, but he began to cry. 'Oh no, don't cry, darling, look, Daddy's come to see us!'

'Don't *want* Daddy,' he whimpered, rubbing his eyes.

'Lucy, put him back to bed, he's tired,' said Mike.

'Oh, he doesn't mean it,' she said. 'Of course you don't, do you, sweetheart? Only *naughty* boys don't want their daddies.' But Mickey was crying in earnest, and he wouldn't stop, even when she told him he was being really *very* naughty. So she had to put him back to bed. Such a pity.

When she returned to the sitting room, Mike was standing with his arms folded. 'This has got to stop,' he said. 'You don't need to walk past my house to get from the school to here. So can you stop doing it, please. You're disturbing my wife.'

'I'm your wife, Mike, your *real* wife. Mickey's your child.'

'For God's sake, I'm not his father,' he said, flapping his hands at her and turning away.

'But you are! That night, Mike.'

'I wish to God that night had never happened,' he whispered, bowing his head. 'I was sorry for you after that break-up, that's all. How many times have I told you? Look, I messed things up, I admit it.' He turned back towards her. 'Lucy, it was one night. You'd been with that graduate guy for months. He must surely be Mickey's father. He even dumped you in bed, didn't he?'

No, no, he was wrong he was wrong he must be wrong! 'He can't be Mickey's father! I've even forgotten his name.'

'Then please try to forget me too, Lucy. I think I'd better go now. I'll let myself out.'

She listened to his feet going down the stairs, to the front door closing behind him. Then she listened to the silence. 'But all you need is one night,' she whispered.

The next morning, after Lucy dropped Mickey at school she walked into the centre of town. She didn't stop until she reached the High Street – the crossing near St Mary's Church which Mike used when he was coming back from his lecture. He'd be here in ten minutes. She had to talk to him again, she just had to.

There were so many people about. The traffic was busy, buses and bikes shooting past her. She began to sweat and feel sick, and her heart was pounding. Mike had to see sense, he *had* to.

She looked at her watch. Nine minutes. She'd walk up as far as the main door of St Mary's and walk back again. Maybe that would make her stop feeling sick.

The third time of walking up and down, she caught sight of him across the street. Only he didn't cross, he carried on up the High Street. No, no, he couldn't! Was it him, though? He had his head down. Oh, she couldn't bear this, he was getting away, and she had to talk to him!

Not taking her eyes off Mike – if it was him – she dashed out into the road.

Somebody screamed, 'Look out!'

She looked up. The bus looked big as it came toward her. So big, so big…

Susan knew now what she was going to do. She looked up from the Oxford Times. 'The driver slammed the brakes on but it was too late. The weird thing is, she just seems to have stood there. "It was like she wanted me to hit her," the driver said.'

'Poor guy,' said Mike. He looked pale. Lucky for him that his lecture had been rescheduled because of a prospective donor's visit, otherwise he'd have been that close to seeing Lucy Granger knocked down and killed.

'Mm… It's the boy I'm sorry for, though,' she said. 'According to what I've heard, the authorities are having a hard time tracking down any family. He's staying with the Daltons – Sammy Dalton is the nearest he's got to a friend. But that's only pro tem. Poor child. It could mean care, I suppose.'

'Yes, I suppose it could. Right, I'd better be off. '

'Do you know, I've been thinking. We've got more space than the Daltons. We could foster him.'

'What?'

'From the glimpse I had of him the other day, he's a child who could do with some family life. And he looked like a nice kid – you know? Jess Dalton's asked me and the girls to tea this afternoon. I'm going to start getting to know Mickey.'

She smiled. Mike's face was a picture. 'Rabbit caught in bus headlights' wouldn't do justice to the way he looked.

CILLA

JOHN KITCHEN

I had to get a Sat Nav.

I'd never needed one in London. I knew the location of my schools there so well I could have found them blindfolded, but with this new post as Primary Advisor in West Oxfordshire, locating the eighty odd schools on my patch was proving to be a major challenge.

Some of them were buried in villages so remote they were never meant to be found by anybody.

I tried googling postcodes and printing off maps, but negotiating country lanes, manoeuvring between the flanks of steaming cows whilst balancing a Google map on one knee put my sanity, to say nothing of my safety, at serious risk. Besides, I was useless at reading maps.

One of my colleagues at County Hall told me there was a special deal on basic Sat Navs in the Botley Road Argos and he thought one of those would suit me fine – and that's how Cilla came into my life.

I named the Sat Nav Cilla after Cilla Black because the voice feeding me instructions was female and had a distinct Liverpool twang; and Cilla was wonderful.

For the first time I was able to appreciate what was around me without the stress of constantly finding myself in remote farmyards with not a hint of an educational establishment in sight. All I had to do was follow her instructions, and I could soak up the acres of farms and fields, and the copses and rivulets; and I could delight in stumbling on schools tucked away in places I could only dream of.

And she understood my navigational dyslexia to perfection.

'After two miles,' she would say, 'enter the roundabout and take the first exit.' Then she would say it again when we were one mile away, and again at five hundred yards. And, as if that wasn't enough, she said it again at three hundred yards and at one hundred yards. Then, because she knew just how stupid I was, she said it all again when I arrived at the roundabout.

I became quite fulsome in my praise. When she got me to some outlandish place I would say, 'You've done a good job, Cilla. No way would I have found this on my own.'

It wasn't all straight forward though. As I got to know the hinterland, I realised that Cilla's advice wasn't always for the best.

For instance, one day, when we were heading for Tackley, a village in the far east of my patch, Cilla's intention was to take me from my house in Curbridge down the A40 to the Peartree interchange.

Knowing what the traffic was like at eight thirty on a Friday morning, I realised that wasn't a good idea.

As we approached the Eynsham roundabout she said, 'After two miles enter the roundabout and take the second exit.' And immediately I said, 'You're not taking me that way, Cilla. We'll be stuck in traffic for ages. We'll take the first exit and cut across to Bladon.'

But she wasn't open to negotiation. When we were a mile from the roundabout she said it again. 'After one mile, enter the roundabout and take the second exit.'

'We're going to take the first exit and go through Bladon,' I said. But at the roundabout she said it again.

'Enter the roundabout and take the second exit.'

'Not likely,' I said. 'I'm taking the first exit and you can go and fry ice.'

She was quiet for a bit after that. Then she said, 'Recalculate,' to which I retorted, 'And about time too.'

All things considered though, it wasn't a bad move having her in the car. Not only did she direct me, but she was someone to talk to and I hadn't had a lot of that since my wife died three years earlier.

She was no great conversationalist but one spring morning she did surprise me.

As I got into the car and eased out of my drive, before saying, 'After two hundred yards turn left,' she said, 'Good morning, Ross.'

I had my head around some problem at the school I was visiting and my brain wasn't entirely in gear. I believe I muttered, 'Good morning,' back. It wasn't until I was heading down the Witney bypass that I was hit by the full import of what had happened.

Had my Sat Nav actually greeted me by name?

I dismissed the idea and decided I'd better start getting out more, but that night as I switched her off she did much the same thing. 'Good evening, Ross,' she said. 'I hope you had a good day,' and the next morning she came up with, 'Did you sleep well?'

I decided I'd inadvertently pressed something and activated a new function.

10

I was surprised that a cheap Sat Nav would have such a sophisticated function, but there was no reason why it shouldn't. Cilla knew the time of day so it was quite feasible for her to greet me in the morning and say good night as I was switching her off, and I knew she was controlled by geo satellites so it was likely she could link up to the Web and locate my name from my email address. She knew my 'home' postcode after all.

I couldn't find any mention of facilities like this when I read the manual, but Cilla could do it so I accepted the fact gratefully. Somehow it gave her companionship more depth.

I soon discovered, though, that she could do even more. I was heading for Kirtlington one day and we were approaching the controversial Eynsham roundabout when she said, 'Do you want to enter the roundabout and take the second exit, Ross, or would you rather enter the roundabout and take the first exit?'

I was stunned, but as I knew she already had additional functions, I decided she must have some kind of inbuilt memory and was adapting to all the recalculation she'd had to make when approaching this roundabout before. I wondered whether they'd programmed in voice recognition too, because, when I said, 'Take the first exit, Cilla,' she came back with, 'OK. Enter the roundabout, and take the first exit.'

From then on Cilla greeted me every morning. She consulted me about the route I wanted to take and, naturally enough, we began to strike up something of a relationship.

It wasn't exactly friendship but, when you've got a 'voice' in the car and it seems to respond to what you say, even when your senses tell you it's all nothing but clever circuitry, you do get into the habit of talking back, and I have to say I liked having Cilla with me.

But she wasn't my only burgeoning friendship at the time.

There was a little school in Northmoor; just a Head and a part time teacher, with a couple of classroom assistants. It was the smallest school on my patch, with only twenty-two children, and it was under threat of closure.

The Head was quite young and very dedicated, but teaching for ninety percent of the week and trying to remain on top of the management and paperwork was hard, and it was my job to support her.

That meant frequent visits and I wasn't averse to them. Debbie Curnow she was called – slight, with dark curly hair and deep sparkling eyes, and I have to admit, I found her evanescent personality most appealing.

Over lunches and coffee breaks we became very easy in each other's company and I really looked forward to my Northmoor visits.

I always kept Cilla switched on when I was driving, even to places like this that were carved into my subconscious. It was company – someone to chat to – someone to confide in… and I did confide in her.

'I've got to admit,' I said one day. 'I wouldn't mind getting to know Debbie Curnow better. She's on her own, you know. Divorced – a couple of 'exes', but… we all make bad choices, Cilla. I mean, you usually don't find out what people are like until you've lived with them for a few years.'

Cilla never replied to these exchanges, but no Sat Nav, however sophisticated, could be expected to, and things were really blossoming with Debbie. There were little treats brought in. She flirted with me, calling me her archangel, her knight in shining armour, and telling me the days I came were her red-letter days.

There was a side to her, though, that made me slightly uneasy.

We were in the staff room one night, working on the School Development Plan when a delivery arrived.

It was a consignment of exercise books.

Debbie had ordered one twenty-five-book pack of each type of book, but somehow the computer had gummed up the order and the delivery lad appeared at the door with a trolley stacked with twenty-five packs of maths books.

It was clear to anybody it wasn't his fault but suddenly, from the charm that she'd been exuding all over me, Debbie changed.

'Is there anything at all between your ears?' she snapped. 'For goodness sake, child, do we look like a school that would use six hundred and twenty-five maths books in one academic year? And I suppose you've got the same number of all the other books out in your van, is that right?' She was glaring at the kid, scorching him with her eyes.

He apologised and explained it must have been a clerical error or a computer glitch, but Debbie wasn't listening. She had the order form in her hand and she was jabbing at it with her finger, sticking it in front of the poor boy's eyes and she was shouting, 'Read that. What does it say? Come on. Read it out loud.'

'It says one pack of twenty-five. It's OK. I'm not disputing it. Like I said, we must have made a clerical error.'

'Quite right you did,' Debbie shouted. 'And you can take this lot straight back, and I'll have the correct order within the week or there'll be trouble. And if you dare invoice me for twenty-five packets of anything, I won't be answerable for what I do. Understand?'

I had to say something. She was so far into the poor boy's face. 'It's not the kid's fault, Debbie,' I said. 'He only delivers the stuff.' And she swung around on me and her eyes were blazing.

'Of course it's his fault,' she snapped. 'If he chooses to work for the company from hell, he deserves to take the flack.' Then she turned back to him and said, 'And you take in what I've told you, young man. I want the correct order and the correct invoice within the week. You can take that message back to the numb-sculls that purport to work in your office.'

The kid was out of there like a cat with a burning tail. And these things are like buses: they all turn up at once because, a few minutes later, she had a call on her mobile and immediately her expression hardened.

She sat there, stony faced, and then she said, 'Well that's typical isn't it? You're as blind as a bat and you've always gone on like you had two left feet.' There was another interval and she said, 'That doesn't surprise me one bit.' After the next pause it was, 'You left it at home? Well you're a bigger fool than I gave you credit for. No! Why would I have your National Insurance number?' Another pause was followed by, 'Well, I suppose I might look if I've got time, but I'm not holding out much hope so don't hold your breath.' Another brief pause was followed by, 'On second thoughts, perhaps it would be better if you did hold your breath,' and with that she flicked off her mobile and turned to me with an indulgent smile and said, 'My ex. The idiot's in Paris. He slipped on a banana skin at Sacré-Coeur and slid from the top to the bottom of the steps. He's broken his leg and the fool's left his Health Insurance card at home. He's labouring under the delusion that I've kept his National Insurance number – as if I would.'

'I don't know, Cilla,' I said as I started up the car that night. 'I've seen another side of Debbie today, and I'm not sure I like it very much.'

I wasn't prepared for a response but her mechanical voice intoned, 'Never mind, Ross. Let's go home.' And it was as if she understood everything I said. It got worse next morning because I didn't sleep much and I was completely out of it. When I switched on the car, the first thing Cilla said was, 'Are you feeling better?' I didn't reply because I couldn't believe I'd heard right. And she came back with

'Hmm! Obviously not!' She sounded quite ratty too and there was no way someone could have programmed a computer chip to say that.

But my head was stuffed. It was the delusion of tiredness. I convinced myself Cilla hadn't actually said anything, and I tried to put her's and Debbie's behaviour out of my head.

I was still captivated by Debbie and I have to admit things were moving at a pace. She invited me back to dinner. She said she'd cook something special and we could crack open a couple of bottles of wine.

When I said we'd better not crack open too many because I'd have to drive home, she said, 'I have got more than one bedroom, you know.'

She was concerned about my map reading skills because she told me she lived at the end of a maze of country lanes. But I was full of confidence.

'I've got a Sat Nav,' I said. 'Just give me the postcode and I'll find you easily.'

The next Saturday I set out, armed with two bottles of the best reds I could find on Sainsbury's shelves and I programmed Cilla with Debbie's postcode.

We turned off in the general direction of Chipping Norton and Debbie was right. We went down a labyrinth of lanes and it took ages.

At last we came to something that looked like a main road and took a left turn into one more lane and finally Cilla announced, 'Your destination is nearby.' Then, 'You have reached your destination.'

I pulled in and glanced around with relief.

To my right there were rolling fields and to my left a stony path. But there was nothing else, other than a cluster of Standing Stones.

'This isn't right,' I said. 'This is the Rollright Stones.'

Then my eyes blacked because Cilla said, 'You're going to see that tart from Northmoor aren't you?'

I was near to meltdown. Either this was some kind of nightmare or, for the last few weeks, I'd been misreading my Sat Nav, and that was an even bigger nightmare.

I couldn't speak. I just grabbed Cilla and re-entered Debbie's postcode. But it was no use. All she did was say, 'I'm not taking you. Postcode not recognised.'

Goodness knows how many miles we were from Debbie's and it was nearly seven o'clock. I was due there at seven.

I switched Cilla off and reached for my mobile, but Debbie's voice was ice-like when she answered. 'How can you be lost?' she said. 'You've got a Sat Nav. Are you sure you put in the right postcode?'

'There's nothing wrong with the postcode,' I said.

I told her we were at the Rollright Stones and I heard her voice turn querulous. 'That's miles away, and dinner's practically ready.'

'Well, what can I do?' I said. 'Can you give me directions?'

There was another pause and then an explosive sigh. 'Have you got a pen and paper? Because you're going to need them.'

Her directions filled a side of A4 and I knew I'd never find it.

I was on the phone again forty-five minutes later.

'I'm still lost,' I bleated.

'There's a dinner here gone to ruin,' she snapped. 'Where are you now?'

When I told her some place called Over Worton, the expression at the other end would have frozen ether.

'Just stay where you are and I'll come out and fetch you,' she barked.

The meat was dry and the sauce congealed. Her soufflé was flat and the pudding tepid and greasy. We didn't consume the wine and I didn't stay the night.

It was curtains for Cilla. The evil little wretch had to go and consigning her to the dustbin was too good for her. She had to be demolished and next morning I placed her, face up, on my patio. I lifted my foot and was ready to bring down the full force of my seventy-six kilos when I heard a terrified little voice.

'What's happening, Ross? What are you going to do?'

I looked down and my eyes were burning. 'I'm going to crush you out of existence,' I growled. 'I want you out of my life.'

'But why?'

'Because you're a corrosive little piece of malice and you're screwing up all my chances.'

I didn't bring my foot down though. I just stood there, balancing with my hand against the wall and I stared at the bit of plastic lying beneath my foot.

'Did I make another wrong choice?' she said, and I could swear the little Liverpool voice was trembling. 'I just wanted to protect you and care for you – to be your best friend.'

I had to get it over with. I tensed my heel, poised for the strike and then, from the ground I heard, 'Recalculate...' and then... 'Oh dear.'

15

And that was too much for me. I bent over and picked her up, and I was hugging her to my chest with tears pouring down my cheeks.

'It's OK,' I whispered. 'I'm not going to hurt you, Cilla.'

I stood there, holding her snuggled to me. But then I heard a voice wafting up with the slightest hint of a Liverpool accent.

'Thank you Ross,' I heard. And then... 'Shouldn't you recalculate with regards that woman from Northmoor now? ... I suggest... turn around... if possible?'

THE SCALE OF THINGS

SHEILA COSTELLO

At the height of summer, if the guest house was full, William would hang a sign on the sitting room door that said, *Residents' Lounge*, place the week's *Oxford Times* by the TV and decamp to the kitchen with Lydia.

The guest house was in a back street in Jericho and it was called Canal View but it didn't overlook the canal, so if you wished to see the water you could either scale the exterior of the building and squat on the roof or you could take a stroll down to the towpath.

Canal View was small. There were two guest bedrooms plus a box room that would magically turn into an additional guest room following a change of duvet and a couple of squirts of eau de cologne. The Residents' Lounge seated five at most. Prices were modest. Lydia prepared breakfast these days. The unfortunate episode with Zoe Vine back in June meant that William kept clear of the cooker. Zoe Vine had had her hash browns done to death and her sausages made to look like the innards of some prehistoric creature by William while Lydia was at the doctor's. She'd cancelled the rest of her stay.

The loss of nearly a week's income meant that from then on William restricted himself to wiping the tops of the ketchup bottles, filling the salt cellars and checking that the plastic sunflowers on the breakfast tables were free of dust. He could do that in his own time when there was no one much about. On the quiet this suited him. He was awkward with people and a close encounter with one of the guests could be a trial. He knew that, as host, he ought to say something but he could rarely think of anything to say. Lydia told him the weather was a safe topic.

'Fine evening,' practised William. Or again, 'Looks like rain.'

Lately though, he'd been spared the ordeal of making conversation. Trade had been slack. Bookings were down, money was tight. People stayed at home and saved cash. He and Lydia had the sitting room to themselves more often than not. Even the regulars were keeping away – Mr Crocker from London who catalogued the flora in the Botanic Gardens with painstaking attention, Mr Crocker who had once mesmerised a fellow guest by dramatising the slow, sticky death of a fly caught on the hairs of a carnivorous plant in one of the greenhouses. Or sad-faced Mr Gorski from Hull who travelled to Oxford to see an old flame and went to Magdalen College for evensong, picking up snatches of ancient melody which he hummed over breakfast next day till the tears drowned his eyes.

Where were they now, wondered William. Shut in their houses, making the morning porridge stretch to cover lunch, scared to turn the heating on if the evenings got chilly? Autumn was well on its way; the future looked uncertain. Lydia was worried about the bills and the mortgage.

Kit Clark rolled up at the end of September. She parked her car somewhere down the road, or possibly round the corner, and said she wanted a bed for the night.

'The weather seems rather changeable,' William answered. 'They talk of storms.'

Kit Clark was short, tawny-skinned and pretty. When she turned her face to him he saw that she had amber eyes. When she smiled he saw that the eyes were flecked with gold. He decided she was thirty-six. She had an air of thirty-six about her. He and Lydia were forty-five. He wished he could think of a little more to say to his guest but he was tongue-tied. He summoned Lydia and disappeared to the shed outside. The neighbours brought their bikes and household gadgets along there to be fixed. He liked fixing things. It provided a bit of extra income as well. There was a mountain bike there today. He got to work but his concentration wandered. It wandered to the thought of Kit Clark's amber eyes. He tried to refocus it on the mysteries of the spanners and screws box. But the eyes had it.

At seven he stopped, perplexed and hungry. He went back to the house.

'Goulash for dinner,' Lydia announced. 'Kit fancies goulash.'

They were all eating together. It was unprecedented. He and Lydia never ate with the guests. But it seemed that in the course of the afternoon Lydia had become quite friendly with the new arrival. The table was set in the small family dining room, not the breakfast room where the guests sat in the mornings, dodging the sharp-edged foliage of the fake sunflowers. And in the centre of the table a candle was lit. Its smoke drifted to the ceiling. State of calm, thought William, trying to subdue his churning stomach. Smoke rises vertically: state of calm on the Beaufort scale.

He'd been extending his knowledge of weather phenomena. It would broaden the scope of his conversation.

Kit Clark walked in. She'd changed out of her jeans and into a smart black dress. She sniffed. 'Something smells tasty.'

William decided that it wasn't him. He smelt of grease and oil. A wash wouldn't be a bad idea. For good measure, while he was upstairs, he took out a blue shirt and a tailored jacket that he wore for weddings and funerals and put them on. Some impulse made him leave the top two shirt buttons open.

'Oh, you've changed too, have you?' said Lydia in slightly aggrieved tones as he strode back in. 'Well, in that case –' She came down five minutes later in a long satin frock.

'You look fabulous, darling,' said Kit. She inspected William. 'And you, you look a picture of manly strength.'

He wasn't sure he deserved the compliment. His face erred on the side of caution. It wasn't a handsome face. His nose was stubby, his eyebrows sparse. He coughed. He wished his heart would steady down. The amber gaze was fixed on him. For the first time in his marriage he realised that he found another woman attractive. He wanted to impress Kit Clark. He cursed his lack of small talk and awkward manner.

'You look fabulous yourself, Kit,' came Lydia's voice.

'Why didn't I say that?' fretted William, and in the same moment realised that he was not the only one with an interest in Kit Clark. Lydia's frock had become a little more décolleté and a bare shoulder was now exposed for consideration. 'What about a drink?' he croaked. 'Let's see what's in the liqueur cabinet.'

'That would be the mop cupboard next to the fridge, would it?' said Lydia under her breath.

'By rights,' said the guest dreamily, 'we should be drinking Hungarian wine and listening to gypsy fiddlers play.'

This cosmopolitan statement made William tremble. He had never encountered Hungarian wine and there were no gypsy fiddlers on their side of the street. At Canal View light classics were the order of the day. He found a bottle of Beaujolais and a CD, *Top Ten Ballet Tunes*.

The guest needed no prompting. She sprang to her feet. 'Dance with me.'

As Lydia put out her hand so also did William. Kit seized the hands of both. With consummate skill she waltzed them round the dining table.

'Such a night,' she laughed. 'Such a night.'

They dug into the goulash, spooning it into each other's mouths, sipping the wine straight from the bottle. Outside the wind began to gust and the branches of a nearby tree creaked and groaned.

'They warned of gales,' murmured William, his thoughts racing. 'Might reach force eight perhaps. Even force ten.'

'Oh, I haven't been in Oxford for so, so long,' laughed Kit. 'I just adore Oxford. The culture, the romance, the beauty of the buildings. I lived here once, you know, in a boat on the canal. I sold jewellery for a living and had an affair with a poet whose golden voice could have stolen your soul. He gave readings in a pub on Walton Street. Scores of people would be there. Afterwards we'd make love till dawn on my little boat, the waters lapping round us.'

Lydia got up, rummaged frantically in a cupboard, produced another bottle of Beaujolais and slugged it down.

'He was a man of diverse and refined tastes,' said Kit. 'He introduced me to the Ballets Russes. What do you think of the Ballets Russes? You have a love of the dance, I can tell. Nijinsky, ah, Nijinsky. What I would give to have seen him on stage. What a genius.'

Lydia executed a pirouette in the centre of the room. She was wildly drunk now. Any inhibitions she might have had were a distant memory. She lifted her skirts, showing a flash of frilly garter and pink sweetheart panties. There was a rasping noise in her throat, like the noise of an animal about to pounce. She arranged herself in a sultry pose on the floor and moaned, 'Oh, Nijinsky was utterly divine.'

William looked away. Nijinsky? Nijinsky who? He'd only just got the Sugar Plum Fairy under his belt and now this. His wife hauled herself into a standing position, tottered to the table and draped her arms round their guest. He felt the need for a change of scene.

'I'm going to make myself a bacon sandwich,' he said.

The spirit of Zoe Vine was waiting in the kitchen. The frying pan caught fire at ten o'clock. A tea cloth went up in flames two seconds later and then a roll of paper towels, a hand towel and the curtains. Smoke swirled round the place. The brigade received an urgent call. Outside the wind reached hurricane strength.

William slept alone that night. Lydia was admitted to hospital suffering the effects of smoke inhalation and Kit Clark simply vanished. When William got back from the hospital around one o'clock, her room was empty and her bags were nowhere to be seen. He didn't know where she'd come from and he didn't know where she'd gone.

She'd left the money for her stay on the dining room table and the precise part of his nature told him that he and Lydia had saved on the cost of her breakfast. He'd heard her murmur as the disaster unfolded in the kitchen that she was on her way to visit a former lover's grave. As the hands of the clock touched half past one he did ask himself if the middle of the night was the best time to go slinking round a cemetery. He couldn't remember whether it was the poet who was supposed to have died or someone else. There had, of course, been others. Anyway, she'd quoted something that she said was from Keats and, blinking her seductive eyes, confessed that she adored romantic ballads.

He'd been overcome. Weak at the knees, his kitchen going up in smoke behind him, he'd gurgled, 'So do I.'

And she had kissed him on the lips.

It didn't matter that he'd seen her do the same to Lydia ten minutes earlier.

He brought his wife home from hospital next day. The damage to her lungs was insignificant. Not so the damage to the kitchen. The blackened walls were just the start of it. It looked to be the definitive end of William's culinary career. He didn't feel too bereft. He'd never really got to grips with cooking. He steered Lydia towards the cupboard and on her lips he planted a passionate kiss. She responded wonderfully, her body melting into his. They kissed again, bruising, burning kisses that went on and on. They both knew what the other was up to. Trying to steal the kisses that their guest had given from the other's lips and make them their own.

Through the window a soft breeze blew and the sky above was clear. Yesterday's storm might never have been. The leaves were changing colour, green giving way to gold and amber. They floated gently from the trees and settled on the grass by the shed.

William snatched another kiss from his wife's eager lips. He felt her pull him towards her and he closed his eyes and smiled. No point dwelling on past mishaps really. Life had its little ups-and-downs. And in the scale of things, just at that moment, the outlook for the future seemed pretty good.

INTO THE OXFORD NIGHT

LIZ HARRIS

Thomas Fitzcairn glanced up from the yellowing pages of the teacher's text book just in time to see a paper aeroplane whiz past Maud's ears and land on the floorboards at the side of her desk. He looked beyond her to Stefan, and saw him smirk as he glanced across at his friends.

He sighed and sat back in his chair. How unfortunate for him that both Stefan and Maud had opted for History that year.

Normally he was anxious to have as many pupils as possible choosing his subject, seeing in them a validation of his teaching skills. But that year he would gladly have had one fewer in the group. The mix of two young people such as Stefan and Maud, both with strong personalities, good leadership skills and the burning ambition to be number one in the class, left much to be desired. It wasn't yet Christmas in the first of the six terms that they were going to be incarcerated together, and he was already bored rigid by their continual squabbling.

He ran his eyes along the faces of the pupils sitting in serried rows in the temporary classroom. He clearly wasn't the only person who was bored that afternoon. He suspected, however, that the tedium of his pupils stemmed from a cause other than the battles between Stefan and Maud.

For yet another day, snow had stopped them from going out in either of the recreation periods. Denied the customary outlet for their youthful energy, they must be longing for the moment when the seemingly never-ending afternoon reached its conclusion.

He looked across to the window at the back of the room, but the snow which had piled up against the grimy panes, obliterated all sense of time. He glanced down at his wristwatch; there was still another hour to be got through before he could set them free. An unenviable prospect if he couldn't get them back on track.

So he had to get them back on track.

Before they slumped into a further torpor, he had to return them to 1142 and make them understand what had happened. A powerful surge of desperation ran through him, taking him completely by surprise.

They had to be made to care about what happened in Oxford all those years ago. Oxford was their home town, after all. It was there, at the castle in Oxford, that Matilda and her supporters were besieged by Stephen for three gruelling months. This was their history, their ancestors, their heritage, and it was up to him to make them forget the lure of the white world outside the classroom walls, even if it was only for a few minutes.

Why he felt overwhelmed by his need to capture the moment for them, he didn't know, and he didn't care. All he knew was that he had to take them back to December 1142.

He got up, went over to the paper aeroplane, picked it up with one of his brown-gloved hands, returned to his desk and dropped the plane into the waste paper bin.

'Put down your pens and any pieces of paper that you're playing with,' he said, sitting down.

He waited for the shuffling to stop, then leaned forward, his chest against the edge of the desk, and stared at the class.

'Let us return to the siege,' he said. 'But this time we will forget our books and let our imaginations do the work. Sit back, close your eyes and forget that you're in a centrally-heated classroom.' He paused a moment, then took a deep breath.

'The night air is raw-cold. We are on the roof of the Tower. The walls enclosing the roof rise nine feet above us. They're pierced on each side by cross-shaped openings. These openings narrow outwards to a slit, keeping us from injury as we stand behind the walls.

A temporary floor has been constructed across part of the roof on beams passed through the walls. Closed in by wooden boards and raw hides, it offers protection to those who drop missiles and burning oil on the enemy below. But there are no soldiers there now. The structure is empty. After close on three months of siege, what missiles there were, are all but gone.

The Empress Matilda moves slowly around the roof, pausing to look first to the north, then to the south, then east, then west. She stares longest towards the west.

But Matilda is not alone on the roof. Standing a little way back from her...

... one of her knights stood watching as she stared towards Oxford, a dark silhouette against a night sky that shimmered red from the fires lit on all sides of the city, so ordered by Stephen as a constant reminder of the guards posted around the castle, who were watching

24

all approaches by day and by night as they waited for the castle's supply of food and fuel to run out.

Matilda leaned closer to the opening in the wall and looked down towards the ground.

The knight stepped quickly forward and took his place at her side, there to protect her should the need arise. Following the line of her gaze, he saw that she was staring at the moat. Covered with a crust of ice, it shone translucent as it bordered the shroud of thick snow that covered the ground.

The churning waters of the nearby mill stream too had been stilled by the cold hand of winter, and its glazed surface reflected the glow of the fires.

The knight glanced across at Matilda.

She must know that the struggle was all but over, he thought, that the day was nigh when she must yield to Stephen and be taken prisoner, when she must give up hope of ever being queen again. What must she be thinking, as she stood there staring at defeat, a proud woman with a fearless heart, and a rightful claim to the throne that she'd fought so hard to make good.

A gust of ice-cold wind cut through him. He leaned back against the wall, cupped his gauntlet-clad hands together and blew hot breath into the cold leather. Then with his left hand, he rubbed the stumps of the three fingers missing at birth from his right hand. A cold blast caught him again, and he shivered and looked longingly at the door that closed off the staircase leading to the lower floors.

Not that the men downstairs were much better off, he thought, wrapping his arms around his body, and trying to hug warmth into himself. It was almost as cold within the castle as without. When he'd left the soldiers below to follow Matilda to the roof, men of all ranks, full of hunger, had been losing hope as they crouched in front of the huge hearth, straining towards the last vestiges of heat thrown out by the dying embers.

For three months now they'd withstood everything that Stephen had thrown at them, but with virtually nothing left to eat, and nothing left to burn as fuel, they had almost reached the limits of their endurance. He knew that, and so must Matilda.

Her sudden movement startled him. She'd turned to him and was pulling her cloak more tightly around her.

'The time has come to act, Tom,' she said.

'You think to surrender, my Lady?'

Her laughter was filled with scorn. 'Surrender to a usurper – I, the rightful queen of England, the only true heir of Henry I? I may have been let down by my father, and betrayed by my cousin, Stephen, but I have not lost my pride, nor have I lost the courage of a true queen. No, Tom, I will never surrender – if not for my sake, for the sake of my son. Henry deserves the chance to be king.'

He inclined his head. 'And king he must be.'

'What say you to the idea of escape?'

He stared at her in surprise. 'Escape? But it's impossible.'

She glanced at the frozen landscape. 'Twice I have defied Stephen; the first time when I succeeded in getting into Arundel soon after my arrival in England, and the second when I fled Winchester during Stephen's siege of the town.' She turned back to him, her eyes glittering in the flickering light thrown by the oil lamp in the corner of the roof. 'What say you that I take my chance for a third time?'

'I say that it cannot be done, my Lady. This is something that I've thought about, but concluded that it cannot be successfully done. There are guards everywhere, closely watching every gate. Your most likely avenue of escape, the postern gate in the tower wall, is watched most closely of all. As for the windows, they are too small to afford a means of escape, and being on the south-west side, you would not easily come outside the castle walls.'

'Then we shall have to find an alternative, shall we not? Take up the lamp and let us return to my men. I wish to have word with several of my knights, and I shall ask you to bring them to me in the lower chamber.'

He inclined his head towards her. 'As you wish, my Lady.'

'I do wish,' she said, her voice steady. 'The time has come for me to bring this siege to an end.'

The four knights stared at her, anxiety etched in their faces.

Humphrey de Bohun stepped forward. 'This cannot be done,' he said, raising his hands in a gesture of helplessness. 'If we are lowered, as you suggest, from the roof of the Tower to the ground below, we shall be seen by Stephen's men for sure. We shall none of us set foot on the ground alive. Such an action means certain death for all.'

Roger Fitzmiles moved to Humphrey's side. 'What Humphrey says is true. We should surely do better to open the gates to Stephen and ask him for clemency. For as long as we are alive, there is a chance that one day you will again be queen, and that one day your son will be king. Your death tomorrow would secure the realm for Stephen, and upon his death for his son, Eustace.'

'I beg you to listen to their words, my Lady,' Miles of Gloucester pleaded, 'and heed them. Your friends speak true.'

'I thank you all for your counsel, but I am decided. My cousin is not a cruel man, yet he must bring my life to an end, should I be captured here. For as long as I live, I shall remain a threat to him. Look around at the devastation that this long siege has wrought; if it continues it will bring about the death of every man here. My choices are three: I can yield to Stephen, I can watch my loyal men die before my eyes or I can flee these walls.'

Tom glanced at the faces of the men around him, and then looked back at Matilda. 'I think you have a plan, my Lady. Night after night you have gone to the roof and stood in the chill air, staring out into the darkness. I have wondered why. I think that now I will have the answer to the question that I dared not ask.'

She smiled at him. 'Yes, I do have a plan, Tom. By night, I have measured the walls with my eyes, and stared towards the villages that lie to the south-west of us. By day I have sat with my ladies and sewn, but we have not embroidered the collars and edges of our sleeves, nor have we sewn jewels on to our chemises; we have been sewing sheets into tunics, white tunics. These are what the four of us will wear. We will merge into the snow, and make the snow an ally in our flight.'

'My Lady, no!' Tom exclaimed. He looked at the other three knights for support. 'You must not take…'

She held up her hand to stop him.

'Tomorrow night, accompanied by Roger, Humphrey and Miles, all of us wearing mantels of white, I shall go by rope down the side of the Tower and make my way to Abingdon, and thence to Wallingford. I have spoken with the local boy who tends our castle fire. He is familiar with the paths and he shall guide us.' She paused and looked at the faces of her soldiers. 'Are you men willing to come with me?'

'We are,' they said with one voice.

'Then we have much to do before tomorrow night. But first, we must rest.'

Tom moved towards her. 'You did not say my name, but I shall come with you. I shall always be at your side, just as my father was before me.'

'No, you shall not, Tom. You will remain behind to return the lamp to the tower when we have gone. We must keep to the pattern of the nights before. Furthermore, we need you here to assist with the terms of the surrender that must be made on the day after we have been found missing.'

'But…'

'You have not the strength in your hands to grip the rope.' She took his right hand in hers and ran her fingers across his stumps. 'God made you thus, Tom. I know that many times in your frustration at your limitations, you have wondered why. We have our answer now. The strength that is missing from your hand has been given to your mind, and you will be serving me well if you use that strength to see that my brave men are spared from any cruel acts of revenge.'

He nodded.

She turned and left the chamber, followed by the three knights. As he stared after them, so great a shiver of apprehension ran through him that he found himself unable to speak.

Stefan thumped his fist on the desk. 'So what happened next, sir? You can't just stop there – it's not allowed.'

'Yes, what happened to Matilda?' shouted Maud. 'I hope she got away. Girl power rules!' She waved her arm defiantly in the air.

'You and your girl power. I bet she was nabbed or killed.'

'That will do, Stefan and Maud, although I must confess to a degree of gratification that you're both so interested in the outcome of our protagonists. But you are right; our story is not yet at an end. Let us move forward to the following night. If you've opened your eyes, I'd like you to close them again. This is something we cannot know as we were not there; we can only imagine it.'

He leaned forward, his elbows knocking against a pile of papers on the desk, his hands clasped in front of his chin. A few of the papers drifted to the floor, unnoticed.

'Imagine what Matilda and her knights must have been feeling as they stood on the roof, knowing that within minutes they would be putting their trust in a thin rope, and would be at risk of striking the sloping stone walls on their descent to the ground.

Imagine what it must have been like for them as they gripped that rope and stepped out into the void, praying that their camouflage stayed in place, aware that if they were caught by the ever watchful enemy, they would be killed.

Think of their relief as they reached the frozen moat and touched it with their feet; think of their fear lest it would not hold their weight, knowing that to slip beneath the ice-bound surface would mean instant death.

How their hearts must have been racing as having left behind them first the moat, then the mill stream, they went forward to meet the challenge offered by the Thames, its thin veneer of ice hiding from view the treacherous undercurrent in the chill waters beneath.

No time for them to rejoice when safely reaching the other side of the solid river, for ahead of them lay miles of ice-hardened marshes, and the increasing risk of capture. How they must have dreaded, every step of their way, that their footprints in the virgin snow would be discovered and that they would be followed by the enemy.

But they weren't.

We do not know why; we can but suppose the reason to be that the wind befriended them and blew fresh snow across their prints, restoring a pristine surface to the white pall that covered the earth.

As we come to the final stages of their journey, it is easy for us to imagine their feelings as they saw ahead of them Abingdon, and knew that from thence they would have horses to carry them to Wallingford – old and weary as they were...

In the distance, a bell sounded.

Disappointment rippled through the classroom.

He looked around at his pupils. 'I'm afraid we shall have to leave the 1140s for the moment and return to the present day,' he said with a regretful smile. 'You may pack your books away and put your chairs on your desks.'

Minutes later, he was alone in the classroom. The muffled sounds that came from the white world outside told him that the inevitable snow fights were already under way.

'In your dreams!' he heard Stefan shout. 'Think you can get away from us, you Maudites, do you? Well, think again.'

Thuds of snowballs finding their mark were followed by screams of delight.

'Come on!' Maud yelled. 'Let's go. He'll never catch us.'

'That's what you think. Who dares, wins!'

Their rivalry faded away into the distance, and silence fell.

As he started to gather together the papers on his desk, he noticed some loose sheets on the floor. He leaned down to pick them up, but the gloves he was wearing made it difficult to grasp them. He sat up, slipped his glove from his left hand, bent down again and picked up the papers.

Straightening in his chair, he put the sheets of paper back on his desk and idly rubbed his gloved right hand with his left hand. It was a relief to have at least one hand free from its woollen covering – wool had a tendency to itch, and to make his hands feel warm and clammy.

He pulled the brown glove from his right hand and felt the fresh air on his skin.

That's better, he thought, and began to rub the stumps of the three fingers that had been missing from his hand at birth.

CHOCOLATE PEOPLE

GINA CLAYE

'Here I am,' I said.
'That's all right.'
'Just for a bit of a sit-down.'
'Whatever you need.'
'You mustn't expect anything from me,' I said, 'I can
only bring a need.'
'Whatever you have.'
Dorothy Nimmo, 1979, Quaker Faith & Practice

Julia clutched her coffee and carrot cake as she searched round for an empty table. Blackwell's coffee shop was full; no doubt everyone was having a well-earned break from the exhausting January sales. That woman was getting up. She darted forward. Drat, now she'd slopped her coffee in the saucer, but she'd got the table. She sank down thankfully, dumped her bag and rehoused the offending slops.

She took a couple of long sips. That was better. Why, oh why had she not got her sister's fiftieth birthday present before Christmas. She knew why: too many Christmas presents to get and the birthday wasn't until the second week of January – plenty of time to deal with it then. She sighed, and put a piece of carrot cake in her mouth. And she'd got nothing to show for her search. She thought she'd cracked the annual problem – a large glass bowl for trifle; she knew her sister wanted one. But she'd tramped round from shop to shop, not one to be seen. 'Sorry,' they'd told her. 'We don't stock them anymore; people tend to buy trifles readymade. There's no call for them these days – although you're the second person who's asked for one this week.'

Weary and wondering what on earth she was going to get her sister instead, she'd given up and sought refuge in Blackwell's Bookshop. She took the hard back book out of her bag. That was the good thing about this place; you could take a book you fancied up to the café with you. *Chocolate Wars* – the name had attracted her immediately. It had been on the stand near the door and she'd scooped it up.

She finished the carrot cake – that would keep her going for a while – and wiped her hands on a tissue; she didn't want to leave any marks. She opened the book with anticipation; the author was Deborah Cadbury. That was really why she'd picked it up – she was a Cadbury Dairy Milk addict. Even looking at the book made her think of a large bar of the chocolate with its purple dust jacket and dark brown covered book underneath. Her mouth watered. She had a bar of the delicious chocolate in her bag. It was the last one of the offer she'd spied – four for the price of two – when she was at the Garden Centre; she just couldn't resist.

She'd finish her coffee first then start on the chocolate, she decided. She opened the book at random. "To address the problem of the product being eaten before it left the factory, a system known as 'pledge money' was put into effect. Each day a penny was awarded to any worker who managed not to succumb to temptation."

Yes, she could see that being a problem. As a child she had raided the garage where her father, who had been a sales person for Cadbury's, had kept his store of Curly Wurlys. Did he realise that some of them had walked? He'd never said.

Apparently, the Cadbury family were Quakers; so were Rowntrees and Frys. She wondered if it was obligatory to make chocolate in order to be a Quaker, whatever that was… all she had come across about Quakers previously was the black hatted man on the packet of porridge oats but recently she'd seen an ad for Quakers on the back of *Private Eye*, featuring a guy who looked anything but stodgy.

She read on, caught up in the story. Outside the clouds gathered and it began to drizzle.

'Have you finished with your plate?' the woman with the green café Nero T-shirt asked.

'Yes thanks,' said Julia moving her coffee cup towards her. She didn't want it taken away before she'd drunk it although by now it was probably luke warm. The afternoon was slipping away and she still hadn't solved the problem of the birthday bowl. Absentmindedly she took a sip of coffee, ugh, it was cold. She pushed the cup away in disgust and dipped into the book again.

"The lid opened to release the richest of scents," she read, "the chocolate fumes inviting the recipient with overwhelming urgency to trifle among the luxurious contents as a whiff of almond marzipan, a hint of orange, rich chocolate truffle, strawberries from a June garden encrusted with thick chocolate beguiled the very air, all begging to be crushed between the tongue and palate…"

This was too much. She must find that last bar of Dairy Milk. She rummaged about in her bag. Why did she keep so much stuff in it? Ah, she had it, no, it was her diary. In exasperation she tipped her bag out into her lap, and gazed in disbelief at the jumble of items, the empty bag and the complete and utter absence of chocolate.

She was sure there'd been one left. She hadn't eaten them all, had she? No. Perhaps it had fallen out in the car when she'd had to slam the brakes on. She needed to get back to the car; thank goodness it wasn't too far away. Luckily she had a friend who lived in Jericho with space in her front garden; the parking restrictions in Oxford were dreadful. And blow the birthday bowl. She'd give *Chocolate Wars* to her sister instead.

Downstairs there were huge queues at all the tills. She waited as patiently as she could, conscious that her back was beginning to ache, and finally handed the book and her credit card to the woman behind the till.

'I'm sorry; this card's out of date.'

Of course it was. The new one was sitting on the dining room table waiting for her to get round to dealing with it. Hastily she pulled out notes and coins from various compartments in her purse. Would she have enough to pay for it? She couldn't bear to think of the trog back into Oxford if she hadn't. Thank goodness. She handed the cash over and put the book in her bag and made for the door.

Outside the drizzle had turned to rain. She pulled up her hood as she walked with the rest of the crowds past the main gates of Trinity College and down the street towards St Giles. Trying to avoid umbrellas held low against the wind, an unwelcome thought struck her. The bar of Dairy Milk wouldn't be in the car; it hadn't been in her handbag at all. She'd put it somewhere so that marauding teenage members of her household couldn't get at it. But where? She couldn't remember. She dodged another umbrella. Was that a newsagent's on the other side of the road? She peered across. It was, and newsagents sold chocolate. A minute later she stepped into the warmth of the shop. There they were – stacks of Cadbury Dairy Milks. With her mouth watering in anticipation she picked up a bar and made for the counter.

Waiting in the queue, another horrid thought struck her. She delved in her bag for her purse. She was right: a twenty pence piece and a few coppers; she'd used up all her money to buy the book. She hunted in desperation in the bottom of her bag and then in both her coat and jeans pocket. No money. She hurriedly put the bar of chocolate back on the shelf and slunk out of the shop.

Did people become utterly depressed through being deprived of chocolate, she wondered as she pulled up her hood again, and hastily decided that she was seriously in danger of being flattened if she didn't get out of the way of the bus bearing down on her. She jostled her way through the oncoming crowd with difficulty. All the world must be out here in Oxford today trying to get a bargain. She negotiated yet another road without coming to harm and started to walk down the side of the Ashmolean. At least it was less crowded here.

She walked past Oxfam and The Eagle and Child. The rest of the walk from here on was a bit tedious. It had been a long, frustrating day and her back and legs were aching badly; how different she would feel if she had a square of Dairy Milk melting on her tongue...

The red door ahead made a colourful change from the grey buildings. Quaker Meeting House it said on the side. Her interest quickened; this was where the chocolate people came... She sneezed suddenly and shivered. Damn, she thought, I hope I'm not going to get a cold. She wished she'd brought her umbrella; the rain was tipping down now and she still had some way to go to get to her car. As she reached into her mac pocket for a tissue, a gust of wind caught her hood and blew it off her head. Icy rain caught her full in the face; it was all too much; she seized the handle of the red door and went in.

It was quiet inside. No one was around. There was a table with leaflets on her left by the door and a large noticeboard on the wall immediately on her right. A staircase led off to the left and the door ahead was open showing a well-stocked library. She pushed her wet hair out of her eyes. At least it was dry in here.

'Hello, can I help you?' The man had appeared out of the library.

'I... I thought I'd just come in.'

'You're very welcome.'

'Thank-you.' Why was she feeling so nervous?

'Do wander around or browse in the library, whatever you want.'

'I don't really want anything.'

'You look as though you could do with a hot cup of tea. I was about to put the kettle on. Will you join me?' Surprised but grateful, she followed him through a room lined with chairs to the kitchen.

'Let me take your mac. I'll hang it up by the radiator, so it can dry off a bit.'

Rather embarrassed she unzipped her mac and handed it to him.

'Thanks. I'm afraid it's dripping all over your floor.'

'Don't worry; it'll soon dry. Take a seat.'

She sat down at the table and dumped her bag which immediately rolled over spilling the book on to the floor.

'Chocolate Wars,' he said, coming over and picking it up for her. 'Deborah Cadbury came and gave us a talk about this book a few months ago. It's a good read – especially if you love chocolate,' he added with a grin.

'Yes, I do and I thought I had a bar of Dairy Milk in my bag, but I didn't and I'm dying for some chocolate.' Why was she telling him this?

'I'll see if there's some in the cupboard. There quite often is. 'No, I'm afraid you're out of luck. Would a cup of hot chocolate do instead?'

'Oh yes, please.' She watched him fill the kettle and switch it on, then reach for the cups.

Her hair was very wet. She could feel odd drops trickling down her face. She pulled some tissues out of her bag and mopped her forehead.

'Here, have a towel.' He pulled one out of the drawer and handed it to her.

'I'm sorry,' she said awkwardly. 'I'm giving you a lot of trouble.'

'No trouble, and if I'm honest, I'm rather glad of the break. I've been re-cataloguing the books in our library and it can get quite tiring after a while.'

She towelled her face and hair dry listening to the soothing sounds of hot chocolate being made. She smoothed her hair down. That was better.

'Here you are,' he said, handing her a large cup and relieving her of the towel.

'Thank-you.'

Relaxing in the warmth of the kitchen and cradling the hot cup in her hands, she watched him sit down and pick up the book from the table.

'You'll enjoy this,' he said.

'Well, actually, it's not for me; I bought it for my sister's birthday but I have dipped into it, and I'm still wondering why so many Quakers made chocolate.'

He laughed. 'A good question.'

'But why?'

'Well, they didn't know how to make chocolate bars at first; that came later. They started by making cocoa drinks as a healthier option to gin.'

Good idea, thought Julia, but then gin had never been her drink. She took another mouthful of the delicious hot chocolate.

'But Cadburys, Rowntrees, Frys – they're all Quakers. Why?'

'Because Quakers were non-conformists, and non-conformists weren't allowed to go to Oxford or Cambridge which were the only teaching schools at the time. That meant that they were barred from the professions. But they had to earn a living.'

'So they made chocolate.'

'Right.'

'They made a lot of money.'

'They did, especially Cadbury's. And they always kept their word so people trusted them and were very happy to do business with them.'

'And George Cadbury built the village of Bournville for his workers.'

'Yes.'

'A village built from chocolate, so to speak.'

'Exactly.'

'Why did he do it?' She took another couple of sips. Mm, this was hitting the right spot.

'Well he, like his fellow Quakers, believed above all that everyone was equal. They were appalled by the slums that children of factory workers were brought up in. They thought everybody, no matter who they were, needed and had a right to proper housing and nourishing food.'

'And gardens.'

'And gardens, 140 feet long, so that they could grow their own veg.'

'Very wholesome.'

'Very, and all built around a green with parks, tennis courts and playgrounds so they could keep fit and have fun.'

'And all because of chocolate.'

'All because of chocolate, and especially Cadbury's Dairy Milk which was very, very popular.'

'It still is,' Julia sighed. She drained her cup, savouring the last mouthful.

'That was what I needed,' she said. 'Thank you.'

'I've enjoyed our chat,' he said, picking up the cups and taking them over to the sink. Julia got up and seized a tea cloth hanging from the rack above the kettle.

It was very peaceful sharing an everyday task looking out over the beautiful silent garden. There was a seat under a tree that looked inviting... perhaps in different weather...

'Any time you want to come and just sit in the garden you'd be very welcome.' He seemed to be able to read her thoughts.

'Thank you,' she said. I'll try and choose a day when it's not raining.' She zipped up her mac, picked up *Chocolate Wars* from the table and put it back in her bag then made for the door.

'You've converted me to hot chocolate – well almost – next to a bar of Dairy Milk. I'm afraid I'm still dreaming about that.'

'Enjoy them both,' he said as he shook her hand and opened the front door.

Outside the cloudburst was over. She stood still for a few seconds then took a long slow breath and started off in the direction of her car. Her step had become lighter; she felt at peace with herself; the world seemed full of promise... Perhaps it was because she felt revived after that friendly meeting in the warm kitchen of the Chocolate House. Certainly it was because she'd just remembered the very unlikely place she'd put that last bar. She'd been in the garden shed – her bolthole when it all became too much – clearing out the clutter ready for spring planting, and there, waiting for her to unwrap it, on top of a stack of seed trays, she was sure she'd find the last bar of Cadbury's Dairy Milk.

The inspiration for this story came from the excellent book, 'Chocolate Wars', by Deborah Cadbury, published by Harper Press. ISBN 978-0-00-732557-3

The Old Jewish Quarter
Oxford, 1265

TURN RIGHT AT FISH STREET

LINORA LAWRENCE

Astranger arrived in Oxford one Tuesday in a particularly windy March. But then Oxford has been used to strangers either passing through or coming to stay even as far back as 1265, when this young man appeared, tired from his journey from Rouen and searching for someone called Isaac in the Jewish quarter.

He stood at the crossroads in the centre of the city. The tower of St Martin's Church was at his back, at the top of the road leading to the castle. The road that had brought him into Oxford was on his left. Common sense told him that the area he was looking for must be near, given the closeness to the castle – that was the way of things in these cities. All he needed was someone to direct him more precisely but he was cautious about whom to ask, given that he was not over-anxious to advertise his arrival.

A young girl emerged, diagonally opposite, from behind a butcher's stall. She stood still and surveyed the scene as if deciding where to go next. She was, perhaps, thirteen, slim with dark hair and bright, intelligent eyes and was modestly dressed. She apparently made up her mind and crossing the road came within a few yards of the visitor.

'*Bonjour*, may I ask you a question?'

She paused, considered and then nodded.

'I have just arrived; I do not know Oxford. I am looking for a man called Isaac. Do you know in which direction I should . . .?' His voice faltered as he wondered if he had after all picked the right person to ask.

'Isaac? There are many Isaacs in Oxford.' Her eyes sparkled as if excited at the challenge. 'Let me see, there is Isaac de Poulet, Isaac de Caen, Isaac of Wallingford and there is Isaac de Coutances.' She paused as she saw the young man react to that last name. She registered that his clothes were dusty from travelling but of a good French cut, his hands were those of a gentleman's and that he stood almost a foot taller than she did. Most of all she noticed his mouth working as he sought for the right words.

'Isaac de Coutances, yes, I think that may be the man I seek. Where may I find him?'

'Go that way,' she said, pointing towards the stalls diagonally opposite. 'Turn right at Fish Street. Go down past all the fishmongers' stalls, past the great stone houses and then, on your left side, you will find Little Jewry Lane. That is where Isaac lives; look for the deer's head on the door.'

'I am most grateful,' said the young man, 'truly. Perhaps I may see you again? I will be staying a while. My name is Aaron.'

The girl bobbed a small curtsy. 'Sir, my name is Miriam and I live in Kepeharm Lane. You will pass it on your way, but on the other side.' Then she collected herself. 'I must go, I have errands to run.'

Aaron watched as she picked up her skirts and made off determinedly in the direction of the North Gate. A lucky encounter and a sweet one – maybe it would bring him luck. He walked off following Miriam's directions. It would have been hard to miss the street given the stink of fish as he did indeed turn right and walk south. Before long he came to some substantial stone houses which instantly reminded him of the better houses in Rouen. The familiarity was comforting. He then turned left and soon found the house with, sure enough, the carving of a deer on the lintel. His knock was answered by a middle-aged woman.

'My husband is not at home,' she replied to Aaron's enquiry. 'He has business with Jacob fils Magister Moses.' She took in the dust and the mud and, most of all, the weariness in Aaron's eyes.

'Do you know when he might return?'

'He is at the castle. It could take all day; it is registration and tax business,' she answered. 'Come in and rest a while. I daresay you could eat a bowl of soup. You may wait for Isaac's return.'

By the time Isaac came home from the elaborate ritual of the opening of the archa chest, in which the roll recording his business had to be deposited, much of the day had gone by. One of the four key holders essential for the ritual had been late. Isaac had walked to the castle with one of the Jewish key holders, Vives le Chapleyn, one of the most important financiers in the city. There they found James of Ewelme on time and awaiting them. However, the remaining Christian key holder was extremely late and all they could do was to wait for him.

Aaron had eaten and indeed slept by the time Isaac came home. However, he was soon alert and anxious to talk about the reason why he had been sent to Oxford to represent his father in a most serious matter.

The next day it rained heavily and Miriam knew she could not avoid getting wet as she set off for Mildegod's house, not that she lived far away, opposite St Aldate's church and next to the synagogue. The rain wouldn't have stopped Miriam in any case; she loved serving the lady, Mildegod, the widow of Copin of Worcester, who continued to run her late husband's business in her own right and was highly regarded in the community.

'Come in child. Make me my drink and come and sit by the fire.'

Miriam obeyed and in a few minutes was warming herself as Mildegod sipped her ale. 'How does your father and your brothers?'

'They do well,' Miriam answered. 'My father keeps the boys very busy.' Too busy to have much time for me she thought to herself. 'I only see them at mealtimes – but they are kind enough towards me,' she added hastily not wanting to give a bad impression. 'It is just that they are anxious to learn the business and to please father, and you know he never stops working!'

'I do indeed,' smiled Mildegod approvingly. 'But your father is happy that you attend me, I think?'

Miriam knew that her father was very pleased that she had found favour with such an illustrious mistress; it was an excellent connection in his opinion. Tactfully, she modified her reply. 'Oh yes, he is very pleased as long as I am at home to make the breakfast and the dinner. They all eat such a lot – at least my brothers do!'

'They have young appetites,' said Mildegod, 'and they are boys. I can remember when I really enjoyed my food. These days I spend my time trying to find something that will relieve my gout. It hampers me greatly. I am trying a new herb today as it happens.'

She paused and then, taking a deep breath, said, 'I have a special task I wish you to undertake, my child. Not today. No, today would be too soon, but in perhaps a week or so. It will involve you going to the castle.'

Miriam stared. What could her task be?

'Don't be nervous; they will be expecting you. I need you to take my seal to the castle. There has been trouble about a document of mine. Someone is disputing my mark so they need to see my actual seal and compare the marks.'

Miriam only half understood, but was very aware that great trust was being placed in her. 'I suppose you cannot go yourself because your gout is so bad at present?' she said, as if it was incumbent on her to offer a possible explanation.

Mildegod grunted. It could have been an affirmative, but she was not committing herself. 'It will be best this way,' she said.

Miriam told her father about the task that evening. He showed some interest. 'Hmm... you would think she would ask her son-in-law, Benedict, to go on her behalf, but then again, maybe she doesn't want him to know about the matter, whatever it is. I'll tell you what, Miriam, when you are told the day I will come with you, walk you to the castle that is. I won't come in because it seems clear Mildegod wants you to go alone, but I will make sure you get there safely.'

Miriam was thrilled at her father's offer, enjoying the parental attention which she had sorely missed since her mother's passing some eighteen months ago. 'What about coming back?' she asked.

'I can't wait about all day,' her father answered, 'but I will think about it.'

And, with that, Miriam had to be content.

Aaron had been invited to stay with Isaac and his wife, Leah, for the time being at least. He was recovering from his travels and feeling more relaxed now that he had arrived safely and been so kindly welcomed. He still carried a considerable weight on his shoulders as he was responsible for a large part of his father's money, but, nevertheless, he now felt able to explore Oxford. Isaac had said it would take a few days to set up the meeting that could now be held because Aaron had arrived. He needed to get to know the city as he might be here for some time. He would walk down one side of Fish Street and up the other learning all the names of the streets and alleys that ran off it. That would bring him back to Carfax where he had met Miriam. It struck him that it would be very nice to have her with him, perhaps able to tell him who lived in some of the houses. He assumed he would see her at synagogue on Saturday, and perhaps Isaac would introduce him to her family.

He came to St. Frideswide's Lane which led to the Priory and then to St. Michael's at the South Gate, beyond which ran the river. He crossed over to what was called Lumbard's Lane with its (to him uninteresting) warehouses. Continuing up Fish Street he came to St. Aldate's church and then Pennyfarthing Lane which did prove interesting. It was the start of a block of Jewish houses which Aaron could identify from the mezuzahs on the doorposts.

Passing Ducklington's Inn he found himself at Kepeharm Lane. It was tempting to look for Miriam but he had a feeling this was not the best way to go about it, so he pressed on past the fish stalls which gave way to butchers' stalls when he came to the cross roads. This area, Isaac had told him, was called La Boucherie for reasons that were all too obvious – the butchers' stalls lined either side of the road and the stench from the blood and the skins was quite simply vile. The road that Aaron had travelled to arrive in Oxford ran east through the city gate, past the Jews' Garden, their burial ground, and over the bridge. To his left lay Great Bayley Street, the way to the castle; straight ahead was the road to the North Gate.

Miriam too had been wondering if she would meet Aaron at the synagogue, though that would only be a glance at each other from the women's section to the men's section. No, everything hung on leaving at the same time and who Aaron might be with.

As it turned out the young were favoured. Aaron was, naturally enough, with Isaac de Coutances. Miriam's father, Samuel Bonefey, and Vives le Chapleyn, had sat next to them. They fell into conversation on the way out and introductions were made. 'This is Aaron d'Evreux,' said Isaac. 'He is in Oxford representing his father, Simon d'Evreux, in the matter of . . . ' he dropped his voice, 'mainperning our old friend, Benedict de Scola.'

'Ah, I see,' replied Samuel thoughtfully. 'Will he be acceptable? He is yet young.'

'I think so, at least I hope so. Everyone knows his father is a wealthy man and also that his health prevents him from travelling. I am sure his son is more important to him than any number of bags of gold, so what better guarantor to offer?'

'It's unusual,' said Vives, 'but it may work. Of course it's not just the other three; the court has to accept his name.'

The women had now come out from their side of the synagogue. Mildegod was surrounded by her friends and Miriam was talking to a girl of her own age. After a few minutes Mildegod detached herself from her group and beckoned Miriam aside. Her father observed this and then noticed Mildegod stoop to whisper in Miriam's ear.

'Was that Mildegod settling the date with you for the visit to the castle?' he asked his daughter.

'Yes, father, she wanted to be sure nothing would stop me attending her on Tuesday as usual; that is the day she wants me to go to the castle – in the morning,' she added.

'Hmm,' said Samuel, stroking his beard, as he turned back to his male companions. 'Master Aaron may care to assist me in a small task,' he announced, 'or rather assist my daughter. She has to make a visit to the castle on Tuesday morning and I would prefer her to be escorted. I will take her myself but I cannot wait about for, I don't know how long, while she sees to the lady Mildegod's business. Would you, young master come with us and wait and then see Miriam is safely returned to the house of her mistress?'

Aaron was delighted with the trust being placed in him and the arrangement was made.

'The lady Mildegod must think Miriam is protected by her innocence,' Samuel whispered to Vives. 'I suppose she thinks a child, and a girl at that, would never be suspected of carrying anything valuable, but I don't want to take any chances.'

'I quite agree,' said Vives. 'I suspect the worst danger may come from within her own family. She is a wise woman, and very single minded when it comes to business.'

Tuesday dawned and Miriam made her way to Mildegod's to collect the seal and a covering letter. She stared at it in amazement – it was the first one she had ever seen.

Coming out of the house she saw her father waiting for her across the road and immediately felt safe. They walked up to Carfax and turned left for the castle where Samuel had arranged to meet Aaron just before they reached the gates. There was what Miriam was to look back upon as a special moment when her father handed her over to Aaron's care.

Miriam went through the gates and made herself known, as instructed by Mildegod. Aaron kept the gate in his sight and settled down to wait. After the clock at St Martin's had marked the hour passing he began to feel a little anxious but another half hour was to pass before Miriam emerged. Her face was shining with happiness and Aaron could tell, long before she reached him, that all had gone well. It had gone better than Miriam had dared to hope; she had been given a letter to take back to Mildegod with her seal and with the words, 'Your mistress will be happy with the resolution.'

She chattered away to Aaron telling him how she had feared the officers would demand to keep the seal and she would have to return empty-handed and how would she explain that? To be told the letter she was given was a positive answer was beyond her wildest dreams, but it had probably happened because one of the officers knew her to be the daughter of Samuel Bonefey. She described the beautiful seal, 'It was a large bird, maybe a pheasant or even a peacock – I am not quite sure – with a scorpion in its mouth!' Despite her doubt about the bird Miriam had the sense to keep the seal hidden away in her pocket. Like her father, earlier that morning, Aaron stayed on one side of the road and kept his eye on Miriam as she crossed and entered Mildegod's house safely.

'And who was that young man watching you from the other side of the road?'

Miriam jumped as she realised Mildegod had been watching from her window, but she could not stifle her joy.

'All is well,' she beamed, 'at least I think it must be!' She went on to explain as she pulled the seal out of her pocket and returned it to its owner. Mildegod read the letter and breathed a long sigh of relief. She looked up. 'The matter is well settled and you have played your part in it. Now fetch me my drink and something for yourself and come and tell me all about the young stranger.'

So Miriam poured out the whole story and Mildegod pricked up her ears when the family name, d'Evreux, was mentioned.

'Ah yes, my late husband had dealings with his father in the old days before he went back to France. I think you should bring this young man to meet me,' she concluded.

And so Miriam did. The first visit was short and formal. Mildegod asked Aaron many questions about his family and indeed supplied some information herself, her late husband, Copin, having known his parents. A few days later Aaron was invited back for a much longer visit and, on this occasion found himself openly discussing his business in Oxford. He explained to Mildegod that Martin of Woodstock, a man close to the king, had accused Benedict de Scola of threatening him with violence. The men were both holders of archa keys for the Oxford chest kept at the castle, though, of course, Benedict was suspended from his duties at present. All four key holders, two Christian and two Jewish, had to be present whenever the chest was opened and business transacted. Martin had been accused of shirking his duties. Benedict retaliated by saying he had been threatened with violence. Accusations flew back and forth and it ended with Martin demanding that the king protect him from Benedict.

The king was put in a difficult position; he had to be seen to do something, but he did not want to fling Benedict into prison for he had been very obliging over the years with substantial loans. The compromise was to mainpern him. Four men with money had to guarantee that Benedict would go nowhere near Martin up to the date of the trial, on pain of forfeiting a large part of their estates. This meant in practice, taking turns to escort Benedict everywhere he went, a job which had to be shared as each man, in effect, acted as a guarantor for his fellow mainpernors. Mildegod knew of such arrangements. The only question was, would the court accept Aaron in place of his father?

Such was the standing of Simon d'Evreux that the court did accept his son as the fourth mainpernor and so Aaron's duties began. During the times when he was not attending Benedict he made himself useful to Mildegod, to Isaac and, occasionally to Miriam's father. Sometimes he earned a silver penny as a scribe.

Time passed. Nearly three years, in fact, before Benedict's trial finally came to court. To the relief of the community, Benedict was acquitted. Aaron had thus fulfilled his duty and there was no longer any reason for him to remain in Oxford.

Mildegod took it upon herself to talk to Samuel, though she wasn't the local matchmaker.

'It is time your daughter was married,' she told him. 'Aaron d'Evreux is entirely suitable and he has conducted himself excellently in that delicate business. Let them be wed, now in the summer while the travelling is still good.' It went without saying that this would mean Aaron taking Miriam back to Rouen, almost certainly for good.

'Miriam's become a fair cook and she keeps the house well for me and my sons. She would be much missed – indeed you would miss her too.' Samuel glanced sideways at Mildegod to judge her reaction to what he thought was his trump card.

'Nonsense,' retorted Mildegod. 'You don't want her left an old maid and nor do I; it would bring shame on your family. If it's someone good in the kitchen you want, I have a widow in mind I could introduce you to . . .'

Mildegod's seal survives to this day and is in the possession of Magdalen College

Pennyfarthing Lane is now known as Pembroke Street

Kepeharm Lane is New Inn Yard (through the arch at St Aldate's Inn)

Fish Street, sometimes called Great Jewry Street, is now St Aldate's

Great Bayley is Queen Street

La Boucherie is the High Street

The road to the North Gate is now the Cornmarket

Aaron and Miriam married and left for Rouen in the September of 1268; their children were born safely in France. In 1290 Edward I issued a decree expelling the entire Jewish population from England.

PLATFORM 3

CHRIS BLOUNT

'I say, are you alright?'

'It's nothing really. I just feel a little faint; I haven't eaten anything all day.'

'Can I get you a cup of tea and, maybe a ginger nut? I'm a doctor so I really should make sure you're OK before you catch your train.'

'How awfully kind, and how lucky that you're here.'

'Well, I'm at the station every Thursday at this time, should you need a doctor again!'

'I'll try and remember to bring the ginger nuts with me, next time! Do you specialise in reviving fainting women?'

'No, I'm just a GP, nothing special, but every Thursday I come to Oxford to help out a friend who runs a private clinic in the city treating patients who have hallucinations.'

'Hallucinations, how absolutely fascinating.'

'Do you take sugar? And by the way, my name's Alec, Alec Harvey.'

'Alec Harvey, what a lovely name. Mine's Laura, Laura…Well, yes, one lump please…'

Laura had caught sight of the plump woman struggling with her shopping and desperately trying to find her ticket; it could only be Roly-Poly Robbo. This was not the right moment to talk to Roly; to tell the truth, it never was the right moment. What on earth would she think? Laura with a strange man! However Laura explained it, Roly's interpretation would be round the county in hours.

'Laura, how wonderful to see you; what are you doing here? Have you been shopping? You should have told me. I'm absolutely exhausted. I think I'm getting far too old for this and it would make it so much more fun to shop together. Oh, and who is this?'

'Roly, this is Alec, Doctor Alec Harvey. He's been so kind, he stopped me from fainting and bought me a cup of tea and a biscuit.'

'How do you do, Mrs…'

'Robinson, Roly Robinson. My real name is Dorothy but everyone calls me Roly. Strange really, I've no idea why, but Roly's sort of stuck and…'

'Can I get you a cup of tea, Mrs Robinson?'

'Well that's awfully kind… but, oh dear, I think they've called our train; they did say Islip and Bicester Town, didn't they? I'm awful with trains. I can never remember where to get off and Laura, are you coming? It is still Platform 3, isn't it?'

Roly talked incessantly all the way to Bicester Town. Laura kept falling asleep and seeing Alec Harvey across the carriage. She had never felt like this before. This must be one of those hallucinations he'd mentioned. Later, as she walked home from the station, she saw him on every corner in his grey mackintosh and brown trilby. But when she got home, it wasn't Alec who opened the door; it was Eric, the unemotional banker whom she had married thirteen years ago, the man who couldn't control the cat (still being sick in the kitchen) or the cooking (boiling over). If only it were Alec…

When Thursday came, she couldn't disguise her disappointment that he wasn't there when she got off the train, but then he wouldn't be would he? He'd be busy hallucinating or whatever it was. She made her way to the exit – but there was nobody there to take her ticket; instead there was a barrier, a strange new barrier that she'd not seen before that ate tickets and spat them out the other end. Thank goodness that kind young man had stopped to show her how to put her ticket in and help her through.

Outside, the buses were huge and bright red; last week she was sure they were smaller and painted an elegant maroon with apple green interiors. She decided to walk to Carfax and go to Timothy Whites where she knew she could find some of those nice new American nylon stockings. But the streets had all changed; instead of the old railway sidings with the funny old blue signalling box, there seemed to be an enormous glass swimming pool with young people sitting at desks looking out into the street. She must get to Timothy Whites quickly and ask the pharmacist to give her some pills to calm her down.

The traffic seemed to be everywhere and there were no black and white crossings telling you where to cross the road, just a flashing green man, whom she thought meant cross carefully, when he really meant 'hurry up, the lights are changing'. And the students? Why weren't they all wearing sports jackets and ties and brogues? They seemed to be Chinese, Indian, and African and spoke all sorts of languages. She knew they must be students because they were nearly all on bikes, but so many were girls, most of them inappropriately dressed, she thought.

At last she got to Timothy Whites, but now it was called Boots. How confusing! It was much bigger and brighter than she remembered. At first, she couldn't find the pharmacy. Last week, she was sure it was a discreet little desk behind which presided a stern pharmacist with horn rimmed glasses, a white coat over a pinstripe suit with a waistcoat (whatever the weather), and wing collar and tie. The pills were in discreet boxes. Now a pretty young woman was openly discussing what sounded like condescending pills with a teenage girl.

Suddenly she saw him; Alec was walking across the floor, waving a newspaper at her.

'How lovely to see you again; how are you feeling now?'

'Fine, thanks. What a wonderful surprise to see you; what are you doing here? But of course, it's Thursday, I should have remembered.'

'Yes, I have to collect some medication for the clinic. And what are you buying?'

She couldn't bring herself to discuss the nylons. 'Just groceries, not that there's much one can buy with coupons.'

Alec looked puzzled. 'Groceries? In Boots? Surely you mean Sainsbury's.'

'Yes, of course, I'm going there next.'

'Have you time for a coffee? There's a Café Nero round the corner.'

'Café Nero? Do they serve real coffee there, not that awful Camp stuff they serve down at Rosie's?'

'They certainly do a good cup of coffee at Café Nero. Do you come into town every Thursday, Laura... can I call you Laura?'

'Yes, do. I usually come and look around the shops and then I see a film in the afternoon.'

They reached the café and Alec steered her to a table by the window. Laura looked around trying to work out why there were no waitresses in black uniforms and starched white headdresses.

'Perhaps you might like a cappuccino as it's so long since you've had a coffee,' said Alec. 'You'll love all the froth and the chocolate which they sprinkle on top.'

'Chocolate, gosh I had almost forgotten the taste of chocolate. How long has this coffee shop been here?'

'About twenty years I think. Why?'

'Twenty years and I've never noticed.'

Suddenly, she felt really happy for the first time for years, young and frivolous. She started to imagine what it would be like dancing with him in a grand ballroom. She would be wearing a pale blue empire line dress and Alec would be in tails and a white tie.

He had not mentioned his wife. Was he divorced or widowed? She felt she could not enquire further. Alec talked more about his general practice in a village called Cholsey, about fifteen miles south of Oxford. There were two doctors and they needed another partner, preferably a woman. Laura was astonished, but so many things were surprising her today.

'Laura, I would love to go on talking,' said Alec looking at his watch, 'but I fear I am going to miss my train; if I walk fast, I think I'll make it.'

'I'll come with you: it'll do me good to get some real exercise, won't it doctor!'

They reached the station just in time; Laura was very confused by the multiple traffic lights in Park End Street and wondered where the jam factory had gone.

'Can I see you next Thursday, Laura? Maybe we could see a film.'

Laura had never experienced this feeling before, not with Eric, not with anyone. It didn't seem right, but everywhere she looked, she could see students holding hands and gazing into each other's eyes. Surely, it wouldn't matter, just the once, though she knew in her heart, there would be another time and another…

Next Thursday couldn't come soon enough for Laura but she was quite nervous. What should she wear? Would lipstick make him think she was a vamp? What about the shopping? How was she going to explain to Eric she had not done any shopping? He always asked what she had bought, even though he really took no interest, unless she had been able to buy cheese with the ration book.

She hadn't meant to, but she was already imagining their life together, 'hallucinating' she thought smiling to herself. They could live in the Stationmaster's little terraced house on Platform 3, next to that little café selling fairy cakes and buttered toast. In their front room, they would have those lovely posters with paintings of steam trains racing to Torquay and Bude to remind them of their holidays. And the children, yes, definitely, two children, Stanley and Elfrida. And she could go over the bridge every day to that dear little shop selling groceries and be served by that nice man, Mr Marks (or was it Mr

Spencer) and buy her newspaper from that charming newsagent with his name above the door, Mr WH Smith...

They watched the film in silence. Laura was impressed it was in colour; it was *Brief Encounter*, about a man and a woman who had a chance meeting at a railway station and then fell in love. It all seemed so improbable...

Alec seemed distracted. Was he having misgivings? Supposing one of his patients saw him? Surely they would know she wasn't... what was her name? Madeleine, yes, Madeleine. Alec had said she was small with black hair. Laura couldn't possibly be mistaken for her. But she was so enjoying herself, and she didn't want to leave the cinema, nor the tea-room they went to afterwards...

Alec broke the silence. 'You know what's happening?'

'Yes. Yes, I do.'

'I've fallen in love with you. Do you feel it too? Tell me it's true. Tell me honestly.'

'No, we can't, we mustn't. We must be sensible.'

'It's too late for that now; too late to be sensible. We both know that.'

'There's still time if we control ourselves,' protested Laura.

They had reached the station by now. Laura put her ticket through the slot in the strange barrier and felt a great sense of pride as the gate opened and let her through.

It was raining hard and his right arm was tightly round her waist. She was excited by this show of intimacy and briefly forgot all the difficulties that could lie ahead, but she was grateful that they walked all the way to the end of the platform, where there were no passengers. Alec kissed her firmly but tenderly and she offered no resistance. Control was clearly wishful thinking, she thought.

'Next Thursday?' whispered Alec.

'Next Thursday,' she said, breathlessly.

Alec wasn't on the platform on Thursday, but she could see him running up the steps as she struggled with her ticket at the strange barrier again.

Oh God, he must think I'm so useless, she thought, but Alec was so thrilled to see her, he didn't seem to notice. 'It's such a lovely day,

I came in by car and I had the hood down, but we shall have to catch the bus to the Park and Ride.'

'Oh Alec, you should have told me; I haven't ridden for years.'

'Gosh, Laura, you don't get about much, do you? The Park and Ride is where people park their cars and take the special dark green bus into the city. There are five of them all round the edge of the city.'

'Five of them,' gasped Laura but didn't want to show her ignorance by saying any more.

She climbed on to the bus at what she thought was the wrong end and the door closed behind her. She remembered running after the bus when she was a child and jumping on to the back step and being helped up by the conductor. But now there did not seem to be a conductor. Alec already had his ticket and he paid her fare to the driver. And how the bus had changed! Some of the seats faced backwards. Still she could enjoy a cigarette while they travelled to the Park and Ride.

'How long is it since you've been on a bus, Laura? You can't smoke here, you know?'

'Well I know some people say it's bad for you and makes you cough, and you are a doctor, of course… but'

'It's more than that; it kills you, and there's also a law forbidding you to smoke on a bus, on the train, in the cinema…'

It was a wonderful day, and they stopped on the bridge by The Trout at Godstow, where he was planning to take Laura to lunch. It was a deep, romantic kiss and Laura thought it would last forever.

Inside The Trout, Laura was expecting spam and didn't believe it was really lamb with fresh vegetables and new potatoes. 'I expect the land girls grew these,' she said. 'I always wanted to be a land girl.'

She thought Alec looked at her a little oddly, but the moment passed.

The afternoon clouded over and it began to rain. Alec closed the hood and Laura was amazed it could be done by pressing a button in the car. It used to take her father about twenty minutes to put all the studs back on his roadster, she remembered, and they all got very wet.

They drove back to the station.

'We have plenty of time for your train.'

They were back in the refreshment room and Alec was buying her a cup of tea...

'Laura, I have to tell you. I am going away. I've got a new job.'

'When? Where?'

'Very soon; I'm going to South Africa…'

'You can't. Not now I need you.'

'Laura, how wonderful to see you; what are you doing here? Have you been shopping? You should have told me. I'm absolutely exhausted. I think I'm getting far too old for this and it would make it so much more fun to shop together. Oh, and who is this?'

'Roly, this is Alec, Doctor Alec Harvey. He's been so kind; he stopped me from fainting and bought me a cup of tea and a biscuit.'

'How do you do, Mrs…'

'Robinson, Roly Robinson. My real name is Dorothy, but everyone calls me Roly. Strange really, I've no idea why, but Roly's sort of stuck and…'

'Can I get you a cup of tea Mrs Robinson?'

'Well that's awfully kind… but, oh dear, I think they've called our train. They did say Islip and Bicester Town, didn't they? I'm awful with trains. I can never remember where to get off and… Laura, are you coming? It is still Platform 3, isn't it?'

'Yes Roly, it is, but no, I'm not coming to Bicester tonight, I'll be waiting for the Cape Town train…'

THROUGH THE MIST OF TIME

HEATHER ROSSER

Ellie hurried along the London Road still fuming after yet another row with her stepfather. She wondered why he couldn't just relax when he returned from his night shift but he always made straight for the bathroom. She had been cleaning her teeth when he hammered on the door. Her cold had kept her awake in the night so she had immersed herself in her library book – a novel set in Victorian times – and overslept.

The wind whipped along the street as Ellie sped away from the tension at home. She was pleased she had decided to cover up today because she was fed up with the way Wayne from IT looked at her legs. She was wearing her long denim skirt with a long sleeved, white blouse over her vest top and a navy jacket she had bought from Primark. She had felt too full of cold to wash her hair that morning so she had scrunched her dark curls into a bun and left the house with the minimum of make-up.

Ellie reached the bus stop as the Brookes Bus slowed to a halt.

'You wouldn't think it was summer, would you?' The woman in front of her looked disapprovingly at the leaden sky.

Ellie shrugged and attempted a smile but her head felt thick and she just wanted to sit down. She brightened when she saw that one of the front seats at the top of the bus was empty and she could enjoy the luxury of an uninterrupted view. They crawled along the busy road and Ellie had plenty of time to watch the children in Bury Knowle Park on the other side of the road. Their bright blue school shirts were a splash of colour on that grey morning as they hurried across the grass towards an adventure playground which had magical carved figures from Narnia among the swings and turreted climbing apparatus. On the far side of the park stood the impressive Bury Knowle House, built of sandstone from Headington quarry. It now belonged to the Council and, among other things, housed the library.

There was a queue of traffic at the zebra crossing by the primary school where a group of children sauntered across the road. A young woman pushing a bike caught up and joked with them as they made their way to the school gate. Ellie guessed that she was their teacher and thought that, unlike her, she seemed to have her life sorted. She blew her nose and looked straight ahead as the bus moved on past Headington shops and towards Oxford Brookes.

When her stepfather had dismissed Ellie's tentative suggestion that she'd like to study history after leaving school he had told her it was time she got rid of her fancy ideas and got a job. However he had agreed to her mother's suggestion that she take a business course. Ellie had imagined doing a business degree at Oxford Brookes University but found herself being pushed into a part-time accountancy course while working for a firm in Botley. Although she had a head for figures, Ellie did not enjoy her job and, as the Brookes students tumbled out of the bus at Headington Hill, she sometimes wondered what it would be like to be one of them. She tried to console herself by thinking about the debt they were accumulating.

Ellie had never had aspirations to go to any of the Oxford University colleges but she loved going past them every day. Unlike some passengers, she was rarely irritated when the bus was held up, and would pass the time looking intently at the ancient buildings in the city centre.

The river was unseasonably high as they crossed the Thames at Osney. Colourful narrow boats were moored along the bank and Ellie wondered how it must have felt to live one's entire life on a boat travelling between Oxford and the industrial Midlands in all weather and seasons. They drove on and past some of the out of town retail outlets – the unadorned cathedrals to consumerism. Ellie rang the bell as the bus rattled over the Seacourt Stream where the city officially ended. Her high heeled boots clattered on the stairs then with a cheery 'Goodbye!' to the driver she walked towards the business park.

By lunch time her cold was worse and she popped into Aldi to buy something to ease the symptoms.

'You look like shit,' said Wayne unsympathetically when she returned.

Ellie scowled and turned her attention to the figures dancing on her computer screen.

'Are you all right, Ellie?' Her boss, immaculate in a Ted Baker jacket, looked at the pile of tissues on her desk with distaste.

'I've felt better.'

'You've looked better, too.'

'Thanks.' Ellie glared at her computer.

'Sorry.' The woman, in her late twenties and armed with a degree in marketing, had the grace to look contrite. 'Why don't you leave

Ellie wondered what sort of discipline she meant. She looked at the children laughing as they queued up for a turn on the swings and noticed that many of their uniforms were worn and patched.

'Do you like your job?'

'Mr Yeates is a fair-minded headmaster and it's better than being a governess.' She put her hand over her mouth, suddenly embarrassed. 'I hope I'm not speaking out of turn,' she said as she scrutinized Ellie's denim skirt.

'Oh no! I work in an office.'

The teacher regarded her quizzically then pointed to a couple of footmen setting up trestle tables and benches in front of the house. 'They'll be having their tea soon; I'll have to go along and see they don't misbehave.'

A boisterous game of cricket attracted Ellie's attention and she began to wander towards the players then paused by a magnificent cedar tree near the house.

'Good afternoon,' she said uncertainly to a couple of middle aged women who were sitting on a bench under the tree.

'Good afternoon,' one of the women replied and patted the seat encouragingly for Ellie to join them. 'Isn't Mrs Ballachey wonderful,' she enthused and pointed to an imposing looking woman in a black taffeta dress who was overseeing the proceedings as the tables were filled with plates of cakes, huge teapots and an enamel plate and mug for each child.

'Such a shame she never had children herself,' the other woman confided.

'She's very forward thinking: she believes that everyone has a right to education,' said the first woman.

'Of course they do,' said Ellie, then wondered if she had said the right thing.

'Yes, of course,' the woman paused, 'as long as they don't forget their station in life.'

'Some do change their situation and better themselves,' her companion said mildly.

Ellie nodded but didn't say anything for fear of giving offence. She watched the headmaster ring the school bell and children run from all directions. There was some jostling as they took their seats but they stopped talking and stared at the dignitaries standing on the steps to the house who in turn looked respectfully at Mrs Ballachey.

The vicar thanked Mrs Ballachey for her hospitality in providing the children's annual treat and for her generosity to the school throughout the year. After he had said grace, the pupils were allowed to tuck into the splendid cake and Ellie smiled as she could see the effort it took some of the younger children not to slurp their tea.

When all the food had been eaten, the tables and benches were taken away in preparation for an entertainment of popular songs and hymns given by the children.

Ellie joined in the enthusiastic applause. Then the pupils were marshalled by their teachers into two lines of boys and girls to walk, crocodile style, across the park. She watched them wistfully then retraced her steps to the flower bed but the friendly gardener was nowhere to be seen. In fact, the flower bed had vanished. Puzzled, Ellie paused and inhaled a lingering scent of lavender. She was once again surrounded by mist but, energised by the perfume, she started walking towards the road. An archway loomed in front of her and she stepped confidently through it.

Children, some in bright blue sweat shirts, were playing; a group of mothers with pushchairs were chatting and people were walking their dogs. Everything seemed normal. She put her hand in her pocket and pulled out a posy of lavender. She glanced back at the big house and smiled with a sudden understanding that things can be different. All the children in the park, past and present, could hold onto the dream of making their life special.

As she reached the street she saw a bus going towards town. She crossed the road and waited at the bus stop.

'Oxford Brookes,' she said, calm in the knowledge that she was taking the first step in shaping her own destiny.

RUIN

ROSIE ORR

*I*t's the way she smiled when I helped her climb in made me do it.

Sort of superior, like – the way she'd smiled that morning when I come to her chamber; I'd been ordered to take the place of her maid, see, who'd taken sick of the palsy during the night. She sighed and fidgeted like a ferret with a flea while I assisted with the robing, tossing her long fair hair about while I struggled to lace up the blue brocade, my chilblains catching on the fastenings; it was all I could do to keep blood off of 'em. When I'd done, I picked the little slippers up off of a nearby cushion, where they'd been arranged just so. Matched the dress, the slippers did, with little twists of gold thread decorating the pointy toes. Love knots.

William, I thought.

William...

The babe kicked as I was kneeling to fit 'em on her feet – it'd been twisting and turning all night; I'd not had so much as a wink of sleep – and before I could help myself I let out a groan. She give me a look would've frozen the Windrush, squeaking in that stupid lisping little voice that if I didn't have a care I'd find myself back in the kitchens again, turning the bloodied boars on their spits. For a moment I thought she'd divined my state, despite the thick folds of the kirtle I'd taken to wearing over my dress – though even if she'd spotted my condition she was as likely to have guessed correctly who the father was as borrowed my wooden pattens to wear instead of the slippers...

Bowing my head humbly, I mumbled something, it being but a gasp of admiration.

Trying not to look at the sweetmeats (the smell of marchpane was making me weak with hunger), I picked up an ivory comb and dressed her hair, pulling as roughly as I dared when I met a tangle. A click of her fingers and I fetched the floral garland, with its snowdrops gleaming like pearls amid the delicate greenery – it made you want to cry just looking at it...

I set it on her head, amid a flurry of instructions to place it just so – *no*, here, *you clumsy sow, not like* that – careful – *careful*, I say! – in order that her newly plucked forehead might be seen to best advantage. I done as I was bid, remembering that summer night in the Dovecote when William spilled mead between my lips warm from his

61

own mouth, and threaded buttercups and daisies in a more private place than a forehead, if you take my meaning…

At last all were gone. I was about to hurry from the chamber when I spied a tiny snowdrop on the floor – it must have slipped from the garland as the bride hastened away and lay there, now, discarded.

Abandoned.

William, I thought.

William…

Painfully I bent, picked it up and slipped it in my pocket, tears bitter as lye falling, till at last even the babe fell still in shared sorrow.

Darkness was falling as I felt my way slowly down the servants' staircase. It was my plan to forage for victuals in the kitchens, but as I neared the Great Hall the sound of merrymaking drew me and despite myself, I crept closer and spied upon the scene from a crack between the painted screens.

Saw the long table, with its richly patterned cloths.

Saw the silver Salt Cellar carved in the shape of a great ship, gleaming in the candle light.

Saw the bridal pair lean towards each other billing and cooing like turtle doves, her with her garland askew and a tipsy slur to her smile, him with a look in his eyes I knew well, a forefinger slowly tracing and re-tracing a violet embroidered on her bodice.

William.

William…

Of a sudden pain clawed at my stomach. I waited for it to pass, but it grew worse, till I could bear it no longer and sank down upon the rushes. When at last I was able, I gathered my strength and pulled myself up. A great time must have passed, for the feasting was come to an end; servants had borne away the great silver platters with their remains of roasted peacocks and gilded calves' heads.

The pain returned, then, and I rested once more. I must have slept a little, for the next I knew the musicians were playing some kind of jig, high and tuneful. Getting clumsily to my feet I applied my eye to the crack once more and saw the company was joined in a dance.

When the prancing came to an end a voice – a stupid lisping little voice – announced that it was tired of dancing and had a mind to play games. Amid laughter and cries of happy agreement – after all, who could deny a bride at her wedding feast? – it was decided that Hide and Seek would commence forthwith.

The Ladyes began to disperse, twittering with excitement, and casting many an inviting backward glance over their shoulders. I moved away, thoughts of the leavings that would be strewn about the kitchen filling my mouth with expectant juices. I had passed the entrance to the Great Hall, and was slipping through the shadows at the bottom of the staircase when a hand shot out and gripped my wrist.

For a moment I thought – hoped...

I turned.

She stood there, scowling. The garland was fading now; there was a smear of honey on her chin, a wine stain darkened the blue brocade. Dragging me closer, as if I was a hound on a chain, she demanded that I show her forthwith to a hiding place so extraordinary that the assembled company would be astonished, and her *husband* – she said the word slowly, tasting it as if it were a spoonful of lemon posset – overcome with admiration at her cleverness.

Perhaps the seeds of what was to come were sown then, in the way she spoke a single word – hitherto, I swear, I'd had it in mind to show her to the Minstrels' Gallery, where she might conceal herself behind the Players. But as she stood there, tapping her foot with impatience, a different idea came upon me.

Husband.

I adjusted the folds of my kirtle to a more becoming drape, smoothed a wisp of hair that had escaped from the cloth that bound it. Lifting a guttering torch from a sconce in the wall, I beckoned her to follow.

Even then, a fright was all my intention as I led her down damp corridors and dismal passages, and – finally – up a little-used staircase. Pushing open a door that shrieked and protested for all the world as if it knew what was to follow, I entered a chamber stacked high with broken furniture and tottering piles of tattered drapes. In the far corner stood a chest of great size, a chest I recalled seeing hauled up the staircase some years ago, but a short time after I arrived at the Hall.

I made my way towards it, almost tripping over a fallen bench – the torch was almost spent now, and shadows leapt and danced in a manner that somehow had me wishing to be gone. Seizing the lid, I pushed and heaved till with a dreadful groan that hid my own gasp as pain ripped through my belly, it opened. I turned, half-expecting My Ladye would have fled by now, but she was already stood beside me, clapping her hands with pleasure like a child. Bending, she seized a baton of wood that I saw had once been part of some ancient chair, and balanced it carefully on the edge of the chest. Lisping that I must take care not to dislodge it when I lowered the lid lest it close entirely, she held out her hand.

Taking it, I helped her perch on the edge of the chest – even in the half-light I could see that her gown was garnished now with dust. She caught my gaze, lifted a handful of brocade and let it fall. Vouchsafed with a smirk that she did not expect to be wearing these rags for long; for if she was not much mistaken, there was room in the chest for two, and when her new *husband* – once more savouring of the word – found her, he would surely… *join her*.

Then, holding tightly to my hand, the pain of my chilblains almost making me cry out, my swollen belly pressing against the rim of the edge till I feared the babe would be expelled forthwith, she lowered herself into the depths of the chest, and arranging herself (as she clearly thought) to best advantage, glanced up at me and smiled.

I cannot tell what thoughts I had when I saw that smile. In some strange way, perhaps none, for before I knew what I was about I had struck the baton of wood from its resting place, reached for the lid and slammed it down. There was an echoing clatter as the iron latch fell into place, followed by a pattering of fists so muffled it might have been the scufflings of mice beneath the floorboards. I stood still for a moment, my mind quite elsewhere, remembering…

As I hurried away, pain clawed once more at my belly and warm liquid doused my skirts. I knew what was to come, and that I must remove at once to the hiding place in the woods I had already prepared, where no-one at the Hall could hear my cries. My travail was not done till the following dawn, my only midwife Mother Moon, my only comfort the branch of willow I bit down on at the last, my agony made easier to bear by the ever more beseeching callings of William and his guests as they searched in vain for the missing bride.

As the sun clawed its feeble way to the top of the beech trees I laid my burden – a tiny misshapen blue-grey creature that never drew so much as a single breath, as different to the rosy babes born to the idle Ladyes of the Household as a rotting windfall to a golden peach – in a hole I scraped beneath a clump of blackthorn. Binding myself as best I could with my head cloth, I made my way back to the Hall, professing great sorrow when I heard the News.

I returned to my duties in the kitchens. Days passed, then weeks, by which time it was generally agreed that My Ladye had gone outside to conceal her person behind one of the great willows that bordered the Windrush, missed her footing, slipped into the rushing waters and been swept away...

Soon afterwards William moved away to London to take up his duties at the Court, and his brother, a man of tastes quite Other, took Guardianship of the Hall. Season followed season, year followed year upon dismal year while I scrubbed and cleaned and chopped and peeled until at last I took sick of a pox that swept through the village one dark winter, and lay forgotten on my pallet till all was done and I was tipped into my grave.

Nowadays, all I once knew and those who followed after them for centuries are gone, and the Hall lies in ruins. But the wind still rustles in the beech trees and the Moon still hangs above the Dovecote, which by some strange fortune alone remains undamaged.

And at last I am happy – for *I* am the Ladye of the Manor now.

I drift about unseen, watching.

Listening.

Perhaps you know some base personage contemplating an indiscretion – a brief dalliance with some maid easily discarded? Will you not encourage him to visit Minster Lovell one summer's eve? Such cunning churls always have a fine time, lazing on the river bank awhile, toying lightly with almond wafers and a pitcher or two of pale wine. Dozing a little till the sun begins to set, casting strange shadows on the ruined walls – shadows that deepen a little as a fitful breeze starts up. If he is like the many who have come before him, he will whisper sweet promises in the foolish girl's ear, suggest a romantic stroll together before they leave...

There will be a sharp chill in the air, now, but the Dovecote is but a short step away; he will easily persuade his companion that it would be a pity to leave without viewing it. Wandering over the springy turf together in the lengthening shadows – stopping, perhaps, to pluck a daisy or two, to ease his way later – he'll exclaim at the faint hooting of an owl, the chiming of the hour from the distant church.

And then he'll push open the door, laughing a little as it creaks and groans – stand blinking in the gloom, suddenly fearful, now that it's too late – *far, far too late* – as it shuts itself with a crash behind him.

Send him soon, I beg.

I'll be waiting.

THE MIDNIGHT PRESS

JANE STEMP

The scullery door was locked, and the front door, but Thomas didn't listen to servants' gossip for nothing. They said the scullery door-frame was so rotten that the tongue of the lock could be levered back with a pen-knife, leaving never a trace behind: and they were right.

He closed the door, hoping that Mr Curtis the apothecary, who lived on the right-hand side, wasn't watching. Mistress Cleeve on the other side would say nothing, even if she did happen to see him. Thomas picked his way across some seeding onions to the gap in Mistress Cleeve's hedge, wriggled under her currant bushes, and made for the passage that led through her house.

Out on Broad Street, Thomas's heartbeat calmed. He took a deep breath of horse-smelling, wood-smoky air, looked carefully around in case of seeing anyone he knew, and crossed to the Turl, where James Fletcher's printing shop was half-hidden inside the old city wall. All at once he had to dodge between two houses and hide; there was Uncle James himself, backing out of the doorway and arguing as he went.

'No, sir, I will not publish your poem: I would not three years ago, and I will not now. Oxford is not the place for it, sir, whatever your Dolbens and Agutters may say. Now, if you will excuse me, I have pressing business.' He pulled the door abruptly shut, leaving the customer inside, and walked towards Northgate with not a glance to spare for the sunshine or the autumn leaves.

Thomas slithered out of hiding, opened the door very carefully, and looked straight – or it would have been straight, if he had not had to look up as well – into the face of a girl about his own age. 'Who are you?' he demanded.

She laced her fingers across the front of her stomacher. 'I am Margaret Rivington, and I might ask the same of you.'

It was one of those moments when Thomas would have liked to be taller. 'You're one of the London book-sellers. I'm Thomas Robinson.' Above the shop, at the head of the stairs, there was a click as the house door opened, revealing a familiar figure: his grandfather.

'Oh.' Margaret wrinkled her nose, but stepped back to let him in. 'Rachel's son. Papa said she married a schoolmaster.'

His father was Master of Magdalen College School, but Thomas let it pass, and peered into the dimness. Uncle James's printing shop was barely fourteen feet square, and the printing-presses took up most of that. As well as Margaret, there was a young man in black, white Geneva bands at his neck, and another man in the corner whom Thomas could not quite make out. 'I'm sorry my uncle was so ungracious, sir,' he said to the young man, who was shifting uneasily from foot to foot and clutching a bundle of papers. 'He was late to meet my family and my other uncle at St Giles' Fair, and he's always cross when he's late. Perhaps he will feel differently about your book when he comes back.'

'I doubt it,' the young man said. 'I had hoped to deal with Mr Fletcher's father, who I believe may be more sympathetic, but I understand he no longer takes any part in the business.' He sighed. 'I had even scraped together the cost of printing the poem myself.'

Thomas looked up to the top of the stairs: his eyes met his grandfather's, which had a distinct twinkle in them. The elder James Fletcher said, in a voice that made everyone else jump, 'Mr Warren, is it not? Perhaps you should have begun with the word "money" to make my son listen. Pray introduce me, sir, to your companion.'

Mr Warren coughed, blushed and said, 'Ah yes, of course. My good friend, sir, Mr Ottobah Cugoano. From London.' He gestured vaguely in the direction of the shadowy figure in the corner of the shop.

Grandfather raised an eyebrow. 'Give me leave to doubt that.'

Thomas stared, trying to look as if he wasn't, at the other man, who stepped forward. 'True enough, sir. But before London, I came from the Fante, in that region of Africa which your people call the Gold Coast. Once I was a slave, but now by the grace of God am a free man.'

Grandfather, astonishingly, bowed. 'As Mr Warren has said, I no longer dictate the business of the shop, but you are welcome, sir. Now, Mr Warren – the same poem, I suppose? But with more money, if I am to believe you.'

The young man gulped, nodded, and seemed struck dumb: but at last he managed to say, 'The same, a little edited. It means so much, sir. To me, and others. Oxford has been lamentably idle in the matter of abolishing the slave trade.'

Thomas's grandfather snorted. 'Oxford is Tory, Mr Warren, and you will know the old rhyme: *Tories own no argument but force.* Leave it to Cambridge to argue the law changed, for 'tis the Whigs who *own no force but argument*. Oxford will go with the law when it changes, believe me, and be content with that.'

Mr Warren drew himself up. 'I will not be content, sir. And I had believed my money might make some difference.'

James Fletcher sat heavily on the top step of the staircase. 'I am an old man, and beyond so much argument. What length is your poem?'

'I have written it out as I would wish it printed, with a preface, and a dedication. It occupies twenty-six pages.' He looked down at the papers in his hands, and held them tighter.

'It were better at twenty-four, but that will be twenty-eight with a half-title. Octavo, I suppose?' Mr Warren shook his head. 'Oh, you poets. Quarto, then, and should have been thirty-two, or sixteen, but no, you will insist on your twenty-eight. And paper costs money, and there are type-setters to be paid, and press-workers and inkers and stitchers. Also I will have no work done in this shop on the Sabbath, and the Rivingtons are Tory to the bone.'

'Not this Rivington, Mr Fletcher.' Margaret curtsied.

'And you, Meg, are a minx.' But his eyes were kindly. 'Also you were pert to my favourite grandchild. Which reminds me, Thomas, why are you not at the fair with the others?'

Thomas braced his shoulders. 'My mother said I should not have spoken back to Uncle William, when I would not sit where he wanted me to. You will understand – it was the room with the paintings of the Dance of Death, and I hate them. So I was told to stay there all evening, but I would not.'

'I do understand,' his grandfather said. 'Death and I are on too close acquaintance these days for me to wish him any nearer. Well, you two young things, and Mr Warren and friend, what shall we do about this wondrous poem?' Nobody moved: and James Fletcher snorted. 'You have yet seven hours to the Sabbath, though all the workers be gone to the fair. I bid you all good day, and do what work you can.' He lumbered to his feet, climbed the last two steps, and closed the door.

'Whatever can he mean?' Mr Warren said.

Ottobah Cugoano said, 'I believe he means us to take matters into our own hands.'

Mr Warren turned a disheartened gaze on him. 'Maybe. But how, God alone knows.'

Thomas took a deep breath. 'God and me. Uncle James made me a toy press once when I was small.' Margaret sniffed, and he added fiercely, 'When I was six! I'm eleven now.'

'And I'm thirteen,' she said: but suddenly smiled at him. 'You're not the only one who can set type. I am a book-seller's daughter, after all. Shall we?'

They stared at one another. '*Can* we?' Thomas said.

'Why did you say so, if not?' Margaret retorted. 'Of course we can, if we use more than one of the presses. Mr Warren, are you willing?'

'I, er, that is – Mr Cugoano, what do you think...?' Mr Warren fumbled with his papers, dropped them, and picked them up again.

His friend was smiling. 'Matthew, chapter 21, verse 16, my friend. "Out of the mouth of babes and sucklings thou hast perfected praise."'

Perfected printing would be more to the point, Thomas thought, but he kept his mouth shut.

'That's settled, then,' Margaret said. 'Twenty-eight pages. We need three sheets and a half for each copy.' She put her hand to her mouth. 'I do hope there is some paper ready.'

'On the cupboard at the stairfoot,' Thomas said. 'Grandfather could see it, I'm sure.' He darted across the room, bumping into Mr Warren on the way, who muttered something about having to be in college, handed a purse and his battered sheaf of foolscap to Mr Cugoano, and blundered out, shutting the tail of his gown in the shop door so that he had to open it again to free himself.

Thomas heaved at the weight on top of the pile of damp paper; it barely moved. Without a word Ottobah Cugoano stepped up behind him, and lifted the weight away.

Margaret leaned over a forme on the table. 'We can use this one. Printed by J. Fletcher in the Turl, and sold by Messrs Rivington. I'll take it apart and re-set the title. What is the poem called?'

Mr Cugoano held the papers close to his face. 'I should remember... ah, yes. It is called, "The Dictates of Indignation. A Poem on the African Slave Trade."'

'Is it a good poem?' Thomas took another blank forme, set it down beside a compositor's table, and unscrewed it.

'It comes from the heart,' Mr Cugoano said, cautiously, and Margaret sniffed again. 'So, not good at all. But the poor man is willing to pay good money to have it printed, so let us give him his wish. Mr Cugoano, will you read it to us, please?'

Thomas never forgot that evening: the twilight darkening outside the cobwebbed windows of the shop, and Ottobah Cugoano's deep voice reading. He ignored the fearful likelihood that eventually Uncle William and the others would come back from the fair to an empty house, and that there was trouble, probably painful trouble, ahead of him. Margaret set one line as it was read aloud, while Thomas read, in his head and backwards, the line he had just set, and slotted the stick of type into the forme. While he set the next line, Margaret read.

Page by page, the seven formes were filled. His finger-tips were sore, and his eyes ached. They lit candles. It took all three of them to set the first two formes in place, and then it was time for the inking. Margaret fetched two printers' aprons, which wrapped her and Thomas from head to toe so that they were swathed like babies and couldn't help giggling. Thomas inked the type. Carefully, carefully, Margaret laid the paper on top, and lowered the platen to cover it. 'Mr Cugoano, will you turn the press, please?'

'Miss Rivington, I shall be delighted.'

'Meg, whatever does he mean by "nefarious merchandise"?' Thomas asked.

Pausing between turns, Ottobah Cugoano answered, 'I suppose, the evil trade.'

'Then why doesn't he just *say* so?' Thomas fielded the paper, turned it over, and laid it on the forme in the next press.

'Because he's a poet,' Margaret said. '*Tom*. Only Mr Fletcher calls me Meg, if you please.' She stepped back to let Mr Cugoano go by.

Thomas shrugged. 'You can call me Tom if you like. I'm not particular.'

Margaret ignored him. 'Thank you, Mr Cugoano.' She slipped the sheet out and hung it over a rail to dry. 'Oh, we have another two sheets to do, and the two halves, and however many copies *will* we be able to print? And after that there's the folding and the stitching.'

'Don't stop to think about it. Have you read that proof?' The three of them pored over the page together, the ink still glistening faintly in the candle-flame. Thomas pointed, careful not to touch. 'Is that how you spell ensanguin'd?'

'Mr Warren spells it that way – Mr Cugoano?'

'Wait – I have the page. Yes, he does.' He was shaking his head. 'Oh dear. This is, truly…'

'It is, isn't it?' Thomas agreed. 'I mean to say, "Float the gay Myriads of the peopled air" – they might be anything!'

'Stop playing the critic, Tom, and go on inking. We haven't all night.'

'Meg the minx,' he muttered, but went on inking.

They worked late, and later than late, until it seemed to Thomas that they had yoked themselves to some invisible machine that made

71

them ink type, and fetch paper, and stand back while Ottobah Cugoano worked the press, then all over again for the other side, and lift the paper off and hang it up; as if they were workers at Mr Arkwright's manufactory in Cromford, and all by candlelight.

'Why are we doing this?' Thomas wondered out loud, when he reached that state of mind where he could do one thing and think of another.

'Because I'm sorry for Mr Warren,' Margaret said. 'And because I'm not like the rest of the family. What about you?'

'I don't know. Because I'm sorry for Mr Warren too, I suppose. But Uncle James is going to be angry as hel… angry as he knows how. Unless Grandfather puts it right with him.' Thomas looked at Mr Cugoano. 'And you, sir, why are you still here?'

'Because of my friend Thomas Warren, and because of the cause,' Ottobah Cugoano said. 'It's good to have two Thomases, and neither of them doubters. Call me Ottobah, my children. I too am not so particular.'

'I doubt lots,' Thomas said. 'But – Grandfather said I was his favourite grandson, and I think he wanted us to do it. So I am, even though it costs me a beating when I go home.' He cast a glance sideways. 'And I don't suppose *she* would have let me run away.'

Margaret was halfway through a yawn. 'Quite right, *you*. How many copies is that?'

'I haven't kept count.'

'Fifty, I think.' Ottobah moved among the lines of wet pages. 'Yes.'

Thomas took one sheet carefully by its corner and lifted it to read a footnote. 'Are you sure people will pay a shilling and six pence to read this?'

Margaret said tartly, 'Maybe not, but they'll pay to be seen reading it, when the cause becomes more fashionable. I'll take these to my room once they're dry. Your grandpapa will help me fold and sew them if I play my cards right.' She lowered her eyes demurely, curtsied, and looked up again: laughter glimmered through her lashes. 'Do you suppose we can get another four copies printed before midnight?' She too picked up a sheet, to read the title page. 'It would have been such a quiz to put Miss Rivington on the imprint, instead of Messrs Rivington. But I suppose that would have put your Uncle James in a rage beyond all bearing.'

Thomas shook his aching fingertips. 'It would. I suppose four more copies won't kill us, if you insist. And if Mr – if Ottobah doesn't mind.'

'Not in the least, Thomas. Onward.'

But they only had two more copies printed when the bells chimed, turn and turn across Oxford, Great Tom last, booming dark as ink across the midnight sky. Another Tom, Thomas thought, and no doubt about the time from him. He untied the apron, and let it drop to the floor. Suddenly he felt as if he was a puppet with the strings cut; floppy, and tremendously tired. 'I'd better go back to Uncle William's,' he said. 'It's been a pleasure to meet you, Ottobah. I hope the other Thomas likes his book.'

'I hope so too,' Ottobah said. 'Miss Rivington…'

'Meg.'

'Meg. Here is Mr Warren's money.' He opened his own purse. 'And if I may give you three shillings in earnest of two copies of the book, I shall be much obliged to you.'

She curtsied. 'Thank you, sir. Ottobah.'

Thomas held the door open for their new friend to leave, and looked back at Margaret, still swathed in her printer's apron. 'See you tomorrow? If they let me out of the house?'

'Before I go back to London, anyway,' she said. 'Don't stand there, Thomas. Your uncle James isn't back yet, so maybe William and the others are still out carousing. If you run they may never know you've been gone.' She smiled at him. 'That is, if you wash the ink off your nose!'

He snorted, shut the door, then opened it. 'Good night, Meg.'

'Good night, Tom.'

He ran back across Broad Street, into the passage through Mistress Cleeve's house and across her garden. The air smelled of wood-smoke still, and mint, when he crushed it on his way through the hedge. Into the scullery once more, after some careful work with his penknife. The paintings of the Dance of Death were waiting for him; but there had been one night of freedom.

Author's note:

In 1791 Ottobah Cugoano, one of the first black British authors, visited over fifty towns in Britain, promoting his book 'Thoughts and sentiments on the evil of slavery'. I like to think that he might have included Oxford in this journey – he certainly knew Sir William Dolben, M.P. for the University. His and all the names in this story belong to real people, but their words and deeds are in my imagination. Except: Thomas Alston Warren's poem 'The Dictates of

Indignation' really was "printed by J. Fletcher in the Turl, and sold by Messrs Rivington". And, in Jackson's Oxford Journal of 7 May 1803, the marriage was announced between Thomas Robinson of Oxford, and Miss Rivington of St Paul's Churchyard, London. William Fletcher, Alice Cleeve and Thomas Curtis, apothecary, lived where the New Bodleian now stands. After 1791 Ottobah Cugoano disappears from the historical record: neither his fate nor the whereabouts of his grave are known.

Thanks are due to the many colleagues on Exlibris-L who helped with my research: in particular, the John J. Burns Library, Boston College, Chestnut Hill, Massachusetts, for providing a scan of the only recorded 1791 copy of 'The Dictates of Indignation'; and Scott Guthery, for sending it to me.

DROP DEAD GORGEOUS

RAY PEIRSON

'Give me some space, please, you stupid man!'

I jumped. I spilled coffee. I hadn't seen her arrive and the rest of the coffee shop was unusually empty. Before I focused on my new neighbour at the table my mild annoyance leaked out, 'Try an empty table if you want space. That's what I did.'

Then I gave her a look, as you do. Then a second look as any man would do. She was beautiful. Even had I not been between girlfriends, I would have taken notice.

To my surprise, she was clearly flustered. Why? My reply though sharp hadn't been out of order. I looked round at the empty tables. After my second look at her I was regretting the words already. Not the best chat-up line, I thought glumly. But, equally glumly, par for the course.

'I'm sorry! I didn't realise that you could hear me,' she replied looking contrite.

I felt bad but my response had already popped out, 'I'm not deaf. Do I look deaf?'

There was a silence. I was confused. She still looked in shock. What had she meant? Of course I could hear her at such close range. We continued looking at each other. I was already consigning any possible continuance to history. There could be no recovery from this disastrous start. Maybe she was your every-day nutter? I was already rationalising the disaster. I looked closer for supporting evidence.

Her clothes were expensive but somehow… wrong… for a coffee shop at mid-afternoon lull. Maybe she had just left a party lasting from the previous evening. This was Oxford after all. Or maybe just the aftermath of a long liquid lunch. If she were pissed, well, it would explain some of it. All of it. Bad news as realistically I couldn't afford ladies who lunched so well they were legless at three o'clock.

I rustled the coffee-shop copy of *The Times* that had become tangled into its usual tabloid-shaped mess and hid behind it like any breakfasting husband. She would hopefully be gone by the end of the Business section, or certainly after the crossword.

'Excuse me?' she said using more reaching-out tones to breach my defences.

I ignored her.

'Excuse me!' Her voice was louder now.

I looked cautiously round the newsprint and raised an eyebrow.

She was crying. Silently. Tears coursing down cheeks. Mascara running. She looked dreadful. She was shaking with emotion. What to do? What to do? I looked round in normal male helpless fashion, hoping rather pathetically for a nearby mature lady to take over. The tables were still spookily empty. Not like Blackwells at all.

My next idea was to abandon the crossword and walk. No, not walk. Run. Then my conscience won the battle and I did the gentlemanly thing. I used my one edge in the gender stakes. I was probably the last man in Oxford under thirty, maybe the world, to own a handkerchief. A large spinnaker-sized one in white. And momentarily Persil clean. I thrust it at her.

She recoiled away from my hand as though fearing violence. The handkerchief lay across the table. The boring brown of cold, spilled coffee was slowly eating into the virgin white.

We were back at the staring at each other situation. What was I getting into here? But common humanity and fear at what she would do if I actually did walk kept me nailed to the seat. Suppose she started screaming? Blackwell's coffee-shop was the centre of my world. I was in publishing after all. They might black-list me for annoying the ladies. Glub!

'Now I know you can hear me, can we have a civilised conversation? I need to talk to someone. Please.'

I nodded. Fine, as long as she didn't make a scene. Or scream. I watched her face as she collected her thoughts. This took some time. I waited. Silence cost nothing. I was working on my exit strategy.

'Do you believe in ghosts?'

Now it was my turn to pause to collect my thoughts. This was a Monday afternoon. I should really be back in the office working on editing a novel about… and I stopped dead. Yes, a novel involving, well not ghosts as such, pretty old hat, but supernatural phenomena anyway. There was only one possible answer. I could see the fear of ridicule in her lovely eyes.

'Yes, of course. Doesn't everybody?'

Her face crumpled. 'Please don't laugh at me.'

'Not,' I claimed insincerely.

'You're humouring me. Please don't. This is too… important to me.'

'OK, my real answer is that ghosts are in the same category as black holes, enemy aliens, Higgs bosons – stuff like that. In short, I don't know. If I can't see it, I don't know.'

She paused almost portentously and said, 'You are looking at one.' She sat back, a gleam of triumph in her eyes, and watched my face carefully. I am happy to say my face was even more blank than usual. I spent a large proportion of my waking leisure hours and my office hours reading genre fiction that could veer off alarmingly into far galaxies, other dimensions and supernatural apparitions. Mad ideas come easily to me which may explain my low-key reaction to all this stuff.

I like to be precise so I said, 'You are a ghost?' Just to pin it down.

She nodded. Obviously ghosts were not overly garrulous. I reached out and retrieved my hanky. It was soggy. She reacted but relaxed when she realised it was hanky-retrieval, not a ghost-testing grope. I raised an eye-brow to demonstrate I had understood her alarm. Everybody knows ghosts are insubstantial.

'I've never done this sort of thing before.'

'You are a trainee ghost?'

'You are laughing at me again?'

'I just like to be precise. How long have you been…?'

'I'm not sure. That is the strange thing. Time is a little… elastic. Or even, backwards. I'm contemporaneous. I'm not from some Jane Austin costume-drama-like past. Unfortunately. I know I have a car licence, or did. You do believe me, don't you?'

I worked on my answer. 'I'm torn two ways. You are beautiful. I would like to do things to you, with you, that need a sense of touch. Apologies for the vulgarity…'

'… Granted!'

'… but ghosts are a little… esoteric… to accept without a firm body of evidence. No puns intended.'

'I'm sure. You mean if I feel a bit… tenuous… to the touch, you'll believe me? Disappointing in the sensuality stakes but proof ghost-wise? But suppose I go pop. Or vanish?'

'Try walking through that wall.'

'You are still laughing at me,' she replied but softened the answer with a smile. I was pretty sure I would find her flesh warm and as pleasingly solid as any girl wants to be.

'Can we move along a bit quicker,' she suddenly said, looking over her shoulder. I followed her gaze but could only see a book-case.

'Sure.' Any direction from here was surely good.

'I need help.'

Were we getting to it, I thought, disappointment hovering in the wings. Was it money?'

'I feel a dreadful sense that something terrible has either happened or will happen to me. Something so awful I can't get my head round it. I need... someone to find out. Otherwise I will be...' She tailed off. Her attention was divided between me and... something else... out of sight. Out of my sight. Not of hers, evidently.

'Look, things are... a little tricky. My name is Susan Verity. I worked in Deacon College. I know it sounds silly but I can't somehow... go... until something is sorted.'

'You want me to find out about your death?'

'I don't think that is it. If I was just... well, dead, I would have moved on to the next...'

'Where?' I said quickly.

'I won't know until I get there, will I? There is something about my... death... that has been left unfinished. I can't look into it.'

'Yes, sure. I can see that. Sorry.'

'Is that too much to ask?'

'Well no, but how can I help you?'

'There must be unfinished business of some sort. How can I know? I can't do anything myself; I'm dead, aren't I? Sorry!' The expression on her face said it all.

'Sure I'll help.' Lies cost nothing. She looked reassured though I couldn't imagine why. Surely she had been out in the world. The Hollywood meaningless promise was not restricted to Hollywood.

'I have to go,' she said flatly.

'Will I see you again?' The words popped out of my mouth though why, I would be totally unable to explain.

'We'll see each other again, somehow. Trust me. I don't know how I know, but somehow I do. Do your best; it is terribly, terribly import...'

She looked fearfully over her shoulder at, past, through the book-case again and... just wasn't there any more. The absence, the silence was as shocking as any explosion of the fashionable terrorist bombs or a head-on car accident.

The evening passed but failed to stick in my memory. I had avoided the office. No problem. The supernatural-inclined book could wait. It wasn't that the sudden invasion of alternative realities was intellectually so disturbing. I had often wished for the boring conventional world to be turned topsy-turvy, the real universe to spring out at me wearing its underpants outside its trousers instead of me just theorising in unengaged intellectual fashion, Oxford-style.

As a publishing exec I understood one thing. It was one of the standard plots I came across in submitted scripts twice a week. Twice a day. The slush-pile was riddled with it. It was a quest. Perhaps Quest with a capital Q was better. Search for the Holy Grail, the sword Excalibur, any damn thing. She had asked, begged, laid a clear duty on me. She had waved a hanky out of the tower and I (on my white charger) would give it my best shot.

I didn't sleep well but was at the office early. I called on my direct line. As soon as I received a sensible response from a young-sounding switchboard it was a clear case of another day, another shock.

'Susan Verity used to work for you. I wonder if there was anybody particularly close to her before she… ah… passed away with whom I could…'

'WHAT!'

'Sorry if you find this enquiry upsetting but…'

'SHE is DEAD?'

'Well, um, yes. She said she… I mean to say… someone, an acquaintance, said she had…'

I heard a confused clatter and murmuring. Clearly the emotional reaction had not faded with time. Maybe her death was recent. She didn't seem sure herself how long…

'WHO is THIS!' This was another voice. Older, strong, annoyed.

'Well, just an acquaintance.' Yes, who exactly was I? And more to the point, why was I?

'What an unpleasant thing to do. I suppose you think this sick joke is funny.'

'I was just…'

'You should see a psychiatrist. If I hadn't seen her pass this office five minutes ago you would have caused such upset. Just get off the line, and don't call again!' The receiver being slammed down hurt my ear.

After a longish period of sitting quietly, my phone rang.

'To whom am I speaking?' inquired a female voice making a civilised business call. I had three dozen a day. Usually from would-be authors wishing to waste my time with great novels. I gave my name.

'I'm not acquainted with you,' continued the female voice in even tones.

I was still not concentrating. I had too much else on my mind. Work could wait. Finally the incongruity of the comment got through to me. 'What?' If she wasn't acquainted with me, why call me? The world was getting weirder and weirder.

'Can I give you my name?'

'Sure,' I said but I was suddenly sure to whom I was speaking. So when the voice spoke the words, 'Susan Verity,' I was unsurprised.

'The very much alive Susan Verity, returning your call. Aren't electronics wonderful? Anonymous calls aren't what they were. What have you got to say?'

Not a lot, was my immediate thought. I didn't even go the mistaken identity route. My ghostly visitation's voice had been distinctive, educated, sexy, unmistakable. This telephone voice, making all due allowances for British Telecom, was distinctive, educated, sexy, unmistakable.

Finally the telephone said, 'Well here I am, still the very much alive Susan Verity. Are you still alive? Speak to me. I am waiting for an explanation.' I could hear a tapping in the background and I was certain it was her toe tapping in fury.

'There is an explanation,' I said in a voice that contained a tad of pleading.

There was a longish pause. The ball was still in my court.

I tried for one exit from my embarrassment. 'Were you in Blackwell's coffee shop yesterday afternoon about three-ish?' There was another silence. I could almost feel her mind working on the appropriate answer. It took a while.

'No, but I will be in Blackwell's coffee shop at three this afternoon. Be there! OK?'

'OK. I'd better describe myself…'

'No need,' she interrupted. 'I'm certain I'll know you immediately. Wild-eyed, slightly, no, totally, bald. Rather, no, very fat. Wearing a badly fitting M&S suit, rather crumpled. With dandruff. And dribbling!'

'Please…'

'Don't worry. You sound too… nice for that description. I would hardly have decided to meet you if I wasn't sure there is some misunderstanding that leaves you squeaky-clean. But I must get to the bottom of this nonsense. I'll describe myself, as logic dictates only one of us needs to recognise the other. I'm…'

I interrupted with a surprisingly detailed description – which stopped her dead, if you'll excuse the expression.

'You've been following me? Are you a stalker?' She seemed intrigued rather than nervous.

'As far as I know I have never met you in my life. Or yours.' She wouldn't understand the caveat.

'Is this the most puzzling phone call of my life? Yes it is,' she answered herself, 'and yet you sound totally sincere. And you have a nice voice, distinctive, educated, and yes, almost sexy.'

'Thank you.'

'De nada.'

I sat myself down in the self-same chair a full half hour before the time. I was quivering but time dragged.

I had got lost in *The Times*, and stuck, in fifteen down, "German Gondoliers in Aspic", when her peach top caught my attention out of the corner of my eye. She was exactly like the girl from yesterday except she was wearing office-type garments and was just a little bit more together in subtle feminine ways.

She had not needed a description of me. She smiled a confident I'm-certain-it-is-you smile. Perhaps I was dribbling. We observed each other for such a long time that in other circumstances would have been intolerably rude. On my side I felt we had been already introduced. Maybe we had.

'Tell me!' she said at last. I hesitated but really if I didn't tell her the truth I had nothing coherent to say. I opened my mouth but she imperiously held up a palm and said, 'Skinny latte, medium, please.' I nodded. She didn't need to explain that I was on probation and all expenses were down to me until I was proved innocent.

I told her the whole story, start to finish. Right up to the ordering of her latte. I sat back. Her eyes perceptibly widened a little at key points in the narrative. She said nothing, however. I fully expected her to stand up at some point, shake her head, and walk silently out. But not.

She sipped gently at her cup and time passed. Eventually she looked up and asked what the… person… had been wearing, a perfectly good female-type question. I tried to describe the dress. I'm a man so I was a little astray at key points but she started adding to my description. It was certainly a high-fashion item. She was looking much more interested now. The dress had to be a real one I realised.

I felt now more emotion than she was demonstrating. It had all suddenly become more real. Somewhere back in a wardrobe was this dress, this real dress. Not one I could possibly have imagined.

She pondered at length. Eventually she said, 'Even if you had been seriously stalking me, had binoculars trained on my bedroom window, whatever, you could not have described that dress. I bought it two weeks ago and the shop alterations are dragging on a little. I was planning to wear it at a dinner party tomorrow.'

'Oh!'

'Exactly, oh! Did I look… nice… in it?'

'Stunning!'

She nodded. 'Good. I was counting on that dress.'

We shared comprehension. We were both intelligent. Perhaps I had read more off-the-wall plots than she had had time for in a busy life but she would have said the logic was plain. I could see the fear in her eyes.

'Let me put the logic of it to you, may I?' she said softly.

'Sure. Of course.'

'Whatever caused me to appear to you yesterday in a dress from the near future has not happened yet. How could it? But how long does a dress, so definitely on trend as that one most certainly is, remain current? Not very long. So how long do I stay current? The logic is harsh. Not very long. She said time was elastic, even backwards, did she? Well, perhaps it is in her situation. Logic dictates that she… I mean me… came to grief in that bloody dress.'

I could see tears in her eyes. I put out a hand as she did simultaneously and we sat like teenage lovers. Except she was now crying. For the second time in two days I was sitting in Blackwells with the same crying lady.

'So you have to be there when I'm wearing the dress. You have to be there to stop whatever it is that killed her… me. I planned to wear it at a dinner party tomorrow night. An old friend of mine promised to introduce me to some bloke she swears is made for me. Some hope, but there you are. Are you up for it?'

Her eyes blazed and knowing she was talking about her own death, what could I say? At the back of my mind I was sure I had something booked for tomorrow night but my diary was mislaid and this was far too important. Scary but important. I nodded again.

We had arranged to meet at her flat. I was there on the dot. She let me in wearing a white fleecy bathrobe and was pink from the shower. The

82

sudden intimacy and the spice of danger made us both conscious of the situation. We had entered the danger zone. The plan was for me to stick close from the moment she was zipped into the dress until the moment she was unzipped.

The plan was to do exactly what she would have done, anyway, but with me four-square beside her. I carried a piece of lead pipe from the old plumbing in my flat in a side pocket. I walked on the outside of the pavement between her and the traffic. I watched above for ropy-looking trees and low-flying helicopters.

There was only one minor incident that momentarily gave me pause for thought. A short, pale-faced man came out of a side-turning rather suddenly. His eyes were staring at Susan. I grasped the lead pipe and tensed but he turned out to be no sort of problem. It was only a scarf in his hand. He saw me and vanished abruptly back into his alley. False alarm. Nothing to worry about.

The tension grew as we neared our destination. I followed her up the path of a very prosperous town house. I had been so busy checking for dangers that it took me a moment to recognise the house. We were spotted from a window. The door opened and my friend John and his wife Maddy looked out at us smiling smugly.

'Great dress, Susan,' said Maddy.

John said to me, 'I've lost my bet. I told Maddy you would forget the invite. You are always doing it.'

Maddy had the match-making expression that married women wear for their friends and said, 'It was Susan I was worrying about. I thought that horrible Oxford Strangler on the prowl might have put her off coming. But you've spoiled things! I was looking forward to introducing you. That is the whole purpose of the dinner party. But you've somehow found each other in some mysterious way without any effort on my part.

'You must be meant for each other.'

THE CREW

ANGELA CECIL REID

The supermarket was almost deserted as Ellie and her trolley arrived at Frozen Vegetables. She had just picked up a pack of Best Buy peas when from immediately behind her came an unmistakable voice. Although she and Martin had only moved to Henley-on-Thames recently, Ellie was already familiar with the terrifying organisational skills of Felicity Russell-Browne.

'Ah, so that's where you've been hiding.'

Ellie turned slowly around. Felicity, a tall, broad-shouldered woman with horn-framed spectacles and several quivering chins, stood just across the aisle.

Relief was instant as Ellie realised that the statement was not directed at her. She shrank gratefully into the shadows beside Organic Oils and Vinegars. This time the victim was Sally Johnston, the vicar's wife.

'Oh, um... h... how nice to see you, Felicity,' said Sally, her eyes flickering towards the exit sign.

Felicity snorted. 'So when are they coming?'

'Are who coming?'

'Goodness, Sally,' snapped Felicity impatiently, 'your crew, of course.'

Sally appeared relieved. 'Oh yes, of course. They'll be here on Saturday, so they'll have ten days training on the river before the regatta.'

'So who'll it be this year?'

'Yale... again. They're a good bunch. We know some of them pretty well now.'

'Darling, I'm sure you do. Sometimes I'm just green with envy. All those hunks around the house.'

'I'm not sure I know what you mean.' Sally's cheeks were tinged with pink.

'Well, all I can say is if you haven't noticed, you're more worthy than Steven deserves.'

'Steven enjoys having them as much as I do.' There was a note of defiance in Sally's voice.

'Well... that extra income must be a bonus.' Felicity smiled, a broad, toothy smile.

Sally's mouth tightened. 'It certainly is,' she said in a voice like broken glass, 'the money goes to a charity of course.'

Felicity's chins quivered apologetically. 'Of course... is it the church roof this time or the refugees again?'

Sally gave a small smile. 'Oh, the refugees. Things are so difficult in their...' Her voice faded as the two women moved off towards the checkout.

Ellie knew almost nothing about rowing, but she did know Henley Royal Regatta was the first week in July. She had walked beside the river each day, and watched as Henley transformed itself into something new, and strangely exciting. Bunting decorated the streets and shop windows were full of straw boaters and elegant hats. Marquees lined the river as far as she could see; a few were blue and white striped, the rest were white. And every day there were more tourists, armed with their cameras and guidebooks. And amongst them moved increasing numbers of oarsmen. Tall, muscular, weather-bronzed, they strode through the crowds like beings from another world.

As Ellie reached the checkout, her mobile vibrated in her pocket. It was a text from Martin. He was reminding her of the task he had delegated to her that morning. She had to find someone to repair their crumbling patio for less than two hundred pounds. Totally impossible, she had thought. But now she had an idea.

Ten minutes later Ellie found herself entering a small office, the door of which was emblazoned with the red and gold words REGATTA ENQUIRIES. A bored looking girl with a halo of ginger curls, sat staring at a computer screen.

'Yes?' she said without looking up.

Ellie took a deep breath. 'I'm interested in putting up a crew for the regatta. How do I go about it?'

That did get the girl's attention. 'It's a bit late in the day, isn't it? Most of the crews got themselves organised months ago.'

Ellie had seldom felt so small. She turned towards the door. The girl's voice stopped her.

'However... I know of a couple of crews looking for last minute accommodation. If you really are interested...?'

Ellie, irritated by the girl's assumption that she was just a time waster, said firmly, 'I am.'

'Well, there's an eight. They'll pay twenty pounds a day each, twenty-five with dinner. The cox will pay less; he won't eat much.'

Ellie wasn't great at maths, but even she could work out that should more than pay for the patio. 'Would they need much room?'

The girl raised her eyebrows. 'We are talking about rowers, not rabbits you know. They'll need somewhere to sleep and shower, and a television. Also a full English breakfast, and mountains of carbs for dinner. Pasta's best, or rice…' she gave Ellie a fierce look, 'and I do mean mountains.'

Ellie had a sudden vision of her immaculate, but small front room in all its subtle tones of beige and Martin in his usual armchair, his swelling belly replete after supper, taking up most of the floor space with his outstretched legs, while one small and eight large young men stood crammed into the corner.

'You said crews. Do you have anything smaller?' she asked, aware she sounded as if she were buying a sofa.

The girl consulted her computer. 'There's a pair from Sydney. Would they suit?'

Ellie did the maths. A pair might still cover the repairs, and even if they didn't, they would make a healthy contribution towards them. 'Perfectly,' she said, suddenly decisive. 'We're in Rose Avenue, Number 5. I'm Ellie Smithers. They can ring me direct to make the arrangements.'

On her return the house was wonderfully silent. Martin would not be home from the brewery for several hours. Ellie loved these times when the house was hers alone. She dared not think too deeply as to why she no longer looked forward to Martin's return from work. Perhaps things would have been different if they had had children.

But this evening, as Ellie hurried about the kitchen, she was filled with an unfamiliar sense of expectation. When the phone rang she was not surprised to hear a young male voice asking her, with Antipodean enthusiasm, if she did really have room to accommodate him and his friend.

She thrust to the back of her mind what Martin would say when he discovered what she had committed him to, and answered warmly, 'But of course. When would you like to arrive?'

She put down the receiver and went thoughtfully into the kitchen. Later that evening, after his favourite supper of fish and chips, Ellie said, 'Martin…'

He grunted and peered at her over the corner of *The Sun*.

'I've found a way to pay for the repairs to the patio.'

'Oh…?' said Martin disbelievingly.

'It was Felicity Russell-Browne's idea,' she lied, knowing how impressed he was by double-barrelled names. 'She suggested we should have a crew to stay for the regatta. They pay well for board and lodging, you know.'

Martin frowned, but the mention of Felicity must have worked; all he said was, 'Where exactly do you think you're going to put them, however many 'them' will be?'

'There'll be just two. I'll clear out the attic; they can sleep on camp beds. I'll even put the old TV in there so they won't have to watch ours. They can use the downstairs shower. In fact you'll hardly know they're here.' This was a remarkably long speech for Ellie, and Martin gazed blankly at her. Before he could think of a reply, Ellie added, 'Oh, and they're arriving the day after tomorrow. Goodnight Martin,' and shut the door firmly behind her.

The following morning as Ellie cleared the rubbish from the attic she reflected that Martin must have been shocked by her display of assertiveness. He hadn't said another word to her the previous night. Nor had he touched her when he eventually came to bed. She was relieved. 'Men have needs,' he frequently told her. 'So do women,' she always wanted to reply, but never had. And now their infrequent couplings filled her only with an aching sense of loss. It all seemed so pointless. When babies had failed to arrive naturally, Martin had refused to explore why.

Ellie was pleased with the result of her efforts in the attic. She was relieved to see that there would be space for two beds, a couple of easy chairs and a table for the television. Filled with a warm sense of achievement she visited the local camping shop. By four o'clock she was satisfied that she had all the essentials. There was now just the food to buy for her crew. She liked the words, 'my crew'; they conjured unexpected, yet pleasurable feelings of control and ownership. But for someone who normally catered for two inactive people, feeding two additional large and hungry mouths was a challenge. It took her into areas of the supermarket and bulk buying she had never explored before.

The following evening her crew arrived. They appeared very tall to Ellie as they ducked through the front door. They were both tanned, and glowed with fitness and health. Momentarily overwhelmed, Ellie forgot to breathe, until one, with a shock of peroxide white hair and eyes of clear sky blue, stepped forward and held out his hand. His grip was hard and warm. Working hands, she thought.

'I'm Zac. Thanks for having us, Mrs Smithers.' He turned towards the second oarsman. 'This is Cooper. He doesn't say much, but he'll turn his hand to most things.'

Cooper was of similar height and solid build as Zac, but his hair was the colour of chestnuts and his eyes were deep brown pools flecked with green. He laughed as he grasped Ellie's hand, 'Zac's right. If you want help, just ask, no probs.'

'Call me Ellie,' Ellie said firmly as she realised how old being referred to as Mrs Smithers made her feel.

She showed them their quarters and waited nervously as they appraised the room; they seemed happy enough if the amount of cheerful banter was anything to go by.

Cooper peered out of the window, 'The view's awesome,' he exclaimed.

Ellie had been surprised by it too when she had cleaned the window the day before. The Thames could be seen beyond the intervening roofs, curving past the water meadows and the gentle swell of wooded hills.

Zac looked across at Ellie, and his eyes really were startlingly blue, 'This'll do us fine. Thanks, Ellie.'

Ellie found that first evening difficult; it was strange having other people there, and Martin was no help. He had come home as usual, and ignored the crew except for a noncommittal grunt when he was being introduced. He soon disappeared to the front room where he ate his supper in solitary silence.

Meanwhile Ellie watched in awe as Zac and Cooper enthusiastically tackled the mountain of pasta she had cooked. As they joked and teased each other, the kitchen seemed a warmer place than it ever had before.

Zac, she decided quickly, was her favourite; his easy laugh punctuated the meal and he was considerate enough to translate the bewildering jargon that peppered their conversation. She learnt of a whole new world where a boat was an eight; a four, a pair or even not a boat at all, but a scull. While an oar was a blade, the stroke was a person, not an action, and feathering had nothing to do with birds or nests. But then Cooper won her over with his delicious lop-sided smile and thoughtful eyes; he was the first to get up to help her clear the table.

That night Ellie took off her glasses and peered into the bathroom mirror. Were those laugh-lines round her eyes, or wrinkles? She feared they were wrinkles, and dabbed on another layer of *Super*

89

Moisture moisturiser. Even worse, were those grey hairs lurking amongst the strawberry-blonde? She sighed. She'd be forty soon. Where had her life gone? A rummage in the bathroom cupboard unearthed a sachet of *Cover All* hair dye and a long forgotten packet of contact lenses.

During the ten days that followed, Ellie had never been so busy, nor so content. The shopping and cooking were a major undertaking. But when Zac and Cooper arrived back from the river each evening, they took turns with laying the table and washing up. She enjoyed their cheerful company.

Martin meanwhile, was hardly to be seen, spending increasing amounts of time each evening in the garden shed.

Wednesday was the first day of the regatta and with great pride Ellie strode along the towpath among the crowds of hats and picnics. As her crew rowed past, their faces contorted in ferocious effort, she screamed her support, and as the loud speakers announced they had won their heat, she cried with joy. As she raced to congratulate them in front of the blue and white striped marquees that she now knew were the boat tents, she passed Felicity Russell-Browne, who gazed at her without a flicker of recognition.

There was a note from Martin on the kitchen table when she returned home. *'Gone fishing. Back Monday'*. Ellie was somewhat surprised. She thought that Martin hated fishing. But the crew would be back soon and starving; there was no time to worry about anything else. The trio spent that evening in a warm cocoon of success.

The next day hope was shattered as two gigantic Irishmen from Killkenny blasted past her pair in the last hundred metres of a tight race. As Ellie looked into Zac and Cooper's exhausted, dazed eyes, she was overwhelmed by a sense of impending loss. Soon they would be gone and her life would continue as before. She shuddered at the thought. Her father had always told her that life was for living, but before the crew had come she had sometimes wondered if she were alive at all.

That evening Zac and Cooper sat in gloomy silence waiting for their supper. Ellie decided she must make it an occasion, and at least try to cheer them up. A hurried excavation in the back of her wardrobe produced a halter neck dress of palest ice blue which she had not dared to wear for years, but which she now slipped over her head. She studied herself in the mirror and this time, with the grey entirely banished from her hair, and the lack of spectacles hiding her grey-blue

90

eyes, she found she was looking at her long forgotten self. A further excavation, this time under the stairs in Martin's wine store, produced a couple of bottles of *Bollinger* champagne.

Zac's blue eyes widened as she came into the kitchen. He smiled. 'The dress's a beaut.'

Ellie felt her cheeks flame red.

'You look awesome,' said Cooper later as he took the heavy pan of rice from her. For a moment he was so close she could feel the warmth of his skin.

'There's champagne in the fridge,' said Ellie feeling suddenly light-headed. 'Can one of you open a bottle? Let's drown our sorrows.'

As the sun sank behind the nearby houses, the boys moved the kitchen table out on to the patio and lit all the candles they could find. When the champagne was drunk, Zac vanished in the direction of the Off Licence, reappearing laden with cans of beer. Disappointment faded, and laughter took its place. Plans for the future were discussed. Zac had a job in banking lined up in Sydney. Cooper was off to work on his uncle's sheep station in the outback, north of Melbourne. Ellie had no plans, and no future, but just then she didn't care. The garden was a magical place, a place outside time.

Later as she lay on the edge of sleep, the bedroom door eased open. Soft footsteps made their way across the floor, a body slid into bed beside her. She lay quite still, unsure if she were awake or dreaming.

'Shall I go?' came the whisper.

'No, please stay,' she heard herself say.

With the lightest of touches her body was teased and caressed, until desire she had only ever imagined pulsed in her blood. Later as strong arms held her close, she fell into deep, dreamless sleep.

It was the dissonant shriek of the alarm clock that woke her. Opening her eyes Ellie saw that she was alone; only the tenderness deep within her told her that last night had not been a dream.

During breakfast she watched the crew intently, searching for clues. Had it been Zac in her bed last night? But he met her gaze with casual friendliness. She turned to study Cooper, but he seemed equally at ease. Later that morning the crew packed their bags and said goodbye. As they kissed her lightly on both cheeks, she searched their faces again. Neither gave anything away.

The house now seemed as silent as death. The large saucepans were put away into the top cupboard. Martin returned on Monday night, followed a few weeks later by a glass case containing a large stuffed carp. He fixed the case to the kitchen wall. Ellie hated the fish's dead eyes and frozen gasping mouth. It made her feel sick. In fact she now frequently felt sick.

Three months after the crew left, she left too. Martin came back to a note which read '*Gone rowing. Back never*'. Ellie had found a job with *Regattas R Us*, a company specialising in water based events, and moved into a small flat in Oxford overlooking the Oxford Canal. During the months that followed, her body swelled.

One soft March morning as cherry blossom petals unfurled and daffodils bobbed in a south-westerly breeze, Ellie gave birth to her son. As she held his small body close to her heart, he opened his eyes and gazed up at her with grey-blue eyes. 'That's no help,' she thought, her mind suddenly half a world away. She smiled. What did it matter? Surely nothing mattered except the child in her arms.

'Hello,' she said, and gently kissed the newest member of the crew.

'Yes,' she thought later as he slept in his cradle at her side, 'life is most definitely for living.' And the future lay spread out in front of her, a glorious patchwork of possibilities.

THE MOTIVATIONAL LISTENER

ALISON HOBLYN

Nicole and Keith were just finishing soy lattes at their window table in Quod; the conversation had stalled, Keith's foot was jiggling up and down and he was scanning the activity in the High. Across the road, at the entrance to the passageway that led to the Radcliffe Camera, he spotted a couple taking photos; they were probably of the same vintage as Nicole and himself and definitely English – there was something about that slightly polite body-language. He was gesturing her to move and pose, which she did with practised smile; in turn she was trying to frame them both in a picture, as nowadays you see the young do, with outstretched arms and hopeful smiles, except that she pondered the results and grimaced.

'Struth, Nicole, those Poms need help.' And Keith bounces through the glass doors and across the path of buses in order to deliver his Australian sunshine.

'G'day mate! Would you like a snap of you and the little lady together?'

Marcus and Fiona smile gently towards the high radiation,

'Well. That's really nice of you.'

'How kind.'

And Marcus delivers the compact little camera into Keith's agitating digits, setting it up so that only 'press' is required. Keith hovers and bends at the knees, aligns and realigns the lens. He knows how to get the best out of people so he relaxes them with his chat. 'Of course, you know I'm a really famous photographer, so this'll be the best pic you've ever seen!'

Marcus and Fiona exchange glances and smile benignly at Keith, holding each other close as she says, 'Do get this signpost in if you can, that would be terrific.'

As Keith hands back the camera, Marcus thanks him.

'No worries mate,' says Keith but doesn't leave it there. He's used to extracting a little reciprocity and just insists that they join him and the wife for a drink; it would be nice to talk to some real natives for both of them. 'And she could do with a bit of company apart from me!'

Nicole is sitting like an island, her long legs crossed as only a woman with slimline thighs can manage; the sun-protected skin of her forearms iridescing gently in the cool light of the interior. She smiles in a professional way, not unfriendly, more as if she was bestowing compassion on stray dogs. The wine is ordered by her – the equivalent of the bowl of water for thirsty mutts. So, there they are, two sets of strangers finding common ground which becomes softer as it's watered by the wine.

'Are you on holiday?' Marcus enquires.

'Not exactly.' It's Keith who talks. 'I'm here on a speaking engagement – but Nicole's just come along for the break, haven't you, love?' He looks at her fondly as though seeking some tacit agreement.

'Yes.' Nicole's swan neck inclines infinitesimally towards him. 'What Keith means is, I've not long lost my Mum. She'd been crook for years then died this spring. This is my first time away since…' she tails off with a scaffolded smile and Marcus smoothly fills the gap. 'I'm sorry – very good idea to get away. And what's the speaking engagement, Keith?'

'Business. I talk about how to persuade and how to get – and hold – a high price. But I'm a story-teller really!' He laughs and Nicole confirms this with a smile and a touch to his arm.

For more than just a few minutes Keith tells them His Story; the beginning in a small mining town in the outback, with Not-a-Lot, through Hard Work going straight from school to the TAFE (with psychology at evening class); starting on the Shop Floor in an engineering business, ('I took to sales like a koala to a gum tree!') and building up a Huge Company; the last chapter being, now the kids were grown, a new career in Motivational Speaking. Keith, accomplished at the downcast eye to go with the self-promotion, simply agreed with Nicole that, yes, he was very well-known in Oz and – short of getting his bank statements out, by the time they'd had a third glass, Marcus and Fiona could surmise that he was paid handsomely for his bon mots.

'I guess it's just because I'm an entertaining, straightforward guy. I mean, I mix with a lot of famous people and they're just happy to be with an ordinary Joe.' With sincere gaze to the middle distance, he adds, 'I like to encourage, to make people feel good – let them know, whatever it is, it can be fixed. It can be better. It can be achieved!' The bottle of Penfolds almost goes flying, but for the quick response of a black-aproned waiter, as Keith's hands swoop like a sea-eagle on the Northern Beaches.

Nicole whispers to Fiona and the two of them rise.

'Where you off to, Nicole? Going to drop the kids off at the pool?!' Keith bellows and laughs. Fiona and Marcus share a bewildered glance as they watch Nicole's glacial body-language but Fiona continues to lead the way to the Ladies. They don't quite look at each other in the mirror whilst applying the lippy; it's then that Fiona takes the opportunity to say, 'I can't know exactly what you're feeling but my mother died a few years ago and I'm just about OK now.' She adds that the last good memory of the three of them together was when they were here in Oxford. 'Strangely, when Keith *leapt* across the road,' (Nicole smiles faintly at Fiona's choice of word,) 'I was trying to get a picture of us under that fingerpost. It was just there Ma said, for the first time, that she could see me and Marcus getting married.' Fiona rubs at her mouth with a finger and laughs 'I said, Ma, are you giving me a sign?!'

'Does it take a long time?' Nicole drops her head to rummage in her bag and Fiona pauses before she says, 'I guess it's different for everyone but it took me about three years.' Nicole nods, seems to shrug off the introspection and addresses Fiona more directly. 'Do you know, I didn't recognise you at first – but it's your voice that's just made me realise. And, I suppose, a few of the looks you got when you walked in.'

Fiona puts her hand out to guide Nicole through the doors back into the restaurant and says, 'Oh, I'm not really anyone except a person who's just having a happy day. Please let's not bother to talk about it?'

And the smiles seal the deal.

'Ah, here are the girls,' says Marcus. 'Fee, I've just this second said to Keith that we're going to visit Woody in College today and what a nice experience that would be for them to come with us, don't you think?'

Keith looks his usual agreeable self; he's agreeable to most things; visiting a student could be good too, especially if it's one of those old, courtyardy places they've glimpsed but not penetrated yet.

Fiona and Nicole both looked pleased enough too and Marcus claps Keith on the back, 'After all, Mr Famous Photographer, one good turn deserves another,' and he pulls out his i-phone to call Woody.

'That's all OK. He'd be delighted to get some tea brewed for us all but he's got a meeting – so we'll have to amuse ourselves till four.'

'How about something really traditional?' says Fiona, 'the chapel at Woody's college has choral evensong.' She does a rather good description of the chapel architecture (because, actually, art history was her subject at university) and watches Keith's very wide but rather polite smile. 'And if we're lucky the choir might be led by Edward Higginbottom; he's very famous – and New College choir have recorded all over the world.' Keith definitely perks up at the word famous.

Turning right down the High they walk past the library of Queen's College and Fiona points out the Britannic figure of Queen Caroline, her statue in a cupola high up on the roofline. They keep heads raised to sight Magdalen Tower ahead of them before turning into Longwall Street. By the time they're in Holywell Street Marcus is walking with Nicole and Fiona is just about keeping up with Keith's energetic pace. They plunge through the bastion walls of New College (which, Fiona tells Keith, is actually not that new – having been founded in 1379. Ha, ha.) She takes them on a small detour into the Fellows' Garden and somehow the intimate enclosure changes the conversation.

'I was saying to Nicole, I lost my mum and it takes a long time to get over that.'

He looks at her. 'Yes. I know. But Nicole's so... I don't know... undemonstrative.' He sighs and lowers himself on to the grass (even then noting it is finer than the stuff back home which feels like a sprung gym floor) while watching his wife on the far side of the courtyard. She is studying some gates whilst Marcus's mouth works away beside her; probably heavily into some historical tirade. 'I mean, I know all the Kubler-Ross stages of grief. And, I don't know, somehow she's got a bit stuck – like a lift between floors. She doesn't cry.' He looks bewildered. 'And I don't seem to be able to Do anything.'

Fiona was quiet for a moment. She could hardly give advice.

'Well, if it helps. What I wanted most was someone to *do* nothing – just listen.'

Keith nods, possibly a little unconvinced.

Marcus is rushing towards them, 'Fee, sweetheart, we haven't noticed the time. Evensong is starting now.' So, heads down, they all scurry through the narrow entry to the Chapel, arriving as the choir are beginning the introit. Shepherded into the rear pews they take their places without the benefit of service sheets and Marcus waves, a tad imperiously, for them to be delivered. Before they are, there is time to simply make sense of the space into which they have been catapulted. Sitting in her straight-backed way, Nicole breathes in a haze of frankincense and feels a suspension of time. The afternoon sun sifts in through stained glass and illuminates the sculpted wall – filled with hundreds of luminaries from centuries past. Fragments of a Catholic school education filter back as she tries to join in the singing with a choir so heavenly it takes her breath from her. As she pieces things together it begins to come clear that this is no ordinary evensong but a service dedicated to the memory of 'the ones who have gone before'; those who have died.

As Keith puts it later, 'I tell you mate, that hit me for six. And I can see it made the little ladies teary.' He looks satisfied as he mutters, 'She'll be 'right.' Walking out through the shadowy cloisters there is distinct lightness as Nicole and Keith link arms. They're laughing as Marcus leads them up a narrow staircase to the Warden's rooms. In the panelled and book-lined space there is set out a sumptuous tea of delicate sandwiches and cakes. 'Oh no, I'm a complete drongo. I thought your mate was a student!' was Keith's comment on being introduced to the effective CEO of the college.

'Easy mistake to make,' Woody says, warmly ushering them to the table. 'Anyway, I'm really nobody – certainly not compared to these two!' He notes Keith's blank expression. 'But, of course, you know that you're in the company of the BBC's National Treasure,' he kisses Fiona fondly, 'and the UK's most respected, war-zone photographer', speaking with a firm shake of Marcus's hand.

This may be the first time in many, many years that humiliation is the visiting emotion for Keith. His mouth gapes and, watching him at such a loss, Nicole puts her arms around him.

'No worries, my darling; look, if you hadn't got up and taken that photo we wouldn't have had this extraordinary day.'

It is hardly discernible through the laughter, especially as Keith now has his head in his hands, but they just hear him say,

'Maybe I should become a Motivational Listener!'

Glossary
Australian into Oxford English
Struth, term of verification or exclamation
G'day, greeting
Mate, general friendly form of address, applied to both sexes

Poms, English folk
No worries, not a problem/it can be solved
Crook, unwell
TAFE, higher education institution
Koala, small Australian marsupial (Phascolarctos cinereus)
Gum Tree, Eucalyptus
Penfolds, well established Australian wine-maker
Sea-eagle, Bird of prey (Haliaeetus leucogaster) resident from India through southeast Asia to Australia.
Northern Beaches, resorts North of Sydney (including Palm Beach where the youth television serial Home and Away is filmed)
Drop the kids off at the pool, to visit the lavatory for a bowel movement
She'll be 'right', things will turn out satisfactorily
Drongo, unintelligent person

COMMEM-O-RAT

RADMILA MAY

Just let me speak, will you? So it was a Commem, one of them fancy balls that students have in the summer, that got trashed. So what? It weren't my fault; it were none of it my fault. Just because you've got a down on us rats. We're persecuted, we are. You humans have got rights, so should we. What we need is a European Convention on Rodent Rights. Who's that laughing? You better not, or you'll be laughing out of the wrong side of your mouth later on, you will. Just give me a chance and I'll tell you my side of the story.

Me and my family, we live in the sewers. We're rats. That's where rats live. You didn't think there was sewers in Oxford? Well, there is, and we have what you might call our ancestral home up in North Oxford where all the posh folk live so I reckon that makes us posh too. Parktown, that's our address, and very nice too.

That night, we was all seated round the dinner table having our tea. Don't ask what it was, you'll only turn all squeamish and start going, 'Yuk, yuk.' You don't know what decent food is, is all I can say. The main thing is, we weren't doing no harm, absolutely none. On my life. Then all of a sudden, just as my dear old mum's pouring out a nice cuppa, there's an almighty crash and a shower of sparks, and I'm lifted out of sight of them all with a whoosh and a bang and whirled away down some dark tunnel. Around and around and along and along. I could have had a nasty injury.

Anyhow, there was a lot of clattering and shaking until I thought all my teeth was going to come out. And then it stops and I'm in the middle of one of them Park and Ride places; you know where they leave the cars and catch the buses into the centre of Oxford. And the first thing I see is some old bat with a pointy hat and wings and a stick in her hand all over sparkles.

'Who are you?' I goes.

'Never you mind,' she snaps.

And then, next to the old bat, who else should I see but that naffing little Cinders. Yeah, that's right. Cinders. Cinderella. Her what's always hanging round. You name it, she's there, moaning and whining about how tough life is. You've never heard the like until you've heard her. Misery Monday, she should be called.

'I know you,' I goes. 'And none the better for it.'

'Ditto,' she says. 'And speak respectful to this lady; she's my fairy godmother.'

'That's a good one. Fairy underpants, more like.'

'Enough from you,' goes the old bat. 'Or I'll turn you into a toad.'

'That'd be an improvement,' sniffs Cinders. Cheek! I thinks, but I don't say nothing. The stick's a magic wand, I reckon. Supernatural powers. That's the worst of these fairy types. Didn't ought to be allowed. But I'll get my own back, see if I don't.

I says to the old bat, all humble-like, 'Beg pardon, madam, but might I inquire what you want with me?'

She waves her wand, all imperious-like, at something behind me. 'You will be driving that.'

'That' is a pumpkin. A bleeding pumpkin.

I says, 'I ain't driving that. It's beneath my dignity. I come from an old family, I do. We don't do pumpkin driving.'

At the same time, Cinders lets out a squawk. 'I can't go in a pumpkin. Not to a Commem ball, I can't. And I can't go with him. He's a rat. He's horrible.'

'Patience, my dear. In the twinkling of an eye it shall be done. But first we require horses.'

And with a wave of that wand and another shower of sparks, like little stars, all at once there's six white mice, all squeaking and tittering and titupping around. You know how mice go on. Then they all stops tituping. They bows low to the old bat and stand waiting, all patient with their little paws clasped in front of them. My dear old mum does a lovely roast mouse, Christmas-time, but that's another story.

The old bat waves that wand. Nothing happens. She waves it again. There's some fizzing and a few pops, then a whole lot of creaks and groans. And then, give credit where credit's due, blow me down if that pumpkin don't turn into a big coach, all white and gold, before my eyes. And those six silly mice into six white horses. Except that instead of horses' tails they've still got their little mice tails. Still, nobody's perfect.

Well, I daresay that's all right for mice. Rodent Rights don't apply to them. But me, I don't fancy being changed in the twinkling of eye, not without my say-so. So I try and make a run for it, but she hauls me back with a wave of that wand. Then I come over all tingly and strange-like. I looks down and stone me, I've got white breeches on and a fancy embroidered coat. And on my head, there's a white wig and a three-cornered hat all over gold braid. I must say, I quite fancy the outfit.

'But what about me?' whinges little Cinders. She's in something white and pink but she ain't happy about it. She plucks at the skirt. 'This is, like, so last year. I can't wear it. Haven't you got anything else, dear Fairy Godmother?'

Well, it was half an hour or more, one dress after another, all them fancy designer labels, before Miss Mona Lott was satisfied. Then there was the fancy handbag. And the shoes. Glass, they was. I knew they'd cause trouble and they did. More of that later.

Eventually we set off and it was smiles all round from little Cinders, kisses, hugs and 'Dear Fairy Godmother, I love you so much.' Huh! Believe that and you'll believe anything.

We rattled down the Woodstock Road, me up top on the coachman's seat and the six white horses trotting along very nicely with a few flicks of the whip, into St Giles and down the Cornmarket. That's one of my favourite streets; all that fast food left lying around. Nice pickings for us rats. But I don't stop.

Up to Carfax, turn left at the lights into the High, then a little way down it's turn right into a small square, then left and we stops outside the entrance to one of them colleges. One of the old ones, what the trippers love, all honey-coloured stone and ivy. I knows it. Leastways I knows the drains and the sewers. High class, they are with a lot of good stuff. I can hear music coming from inside the college. What now? I says to myself.

There's a hammering from inside the coach and Cinders sticks her head out of the window.

'Aren't you going to open the door for me?' she bawls.

I'm not taking any cheek from her. 'Open it yourself, you idle cow.' But then I remember the old bat and her threat to turn me into a toad. So I gets down from my seat and opens the door for her.

She starts to sweep past me like Lady Muck but I grab her arm. 'Get off me,' she shrieks. 'Under all that finery you're still a disgusting old rat.'

'And you, with all your airs and graces, you're still just a little scrubber. Tell me, Miss High-and-Mighty, what's me and all them mice to do while you're in there enjoying yourself?'

She pulls her arm away. 'Why should I care?' She sweeps through the doorway of the college and the doors slam shut behind her, leaving only a smell of the most tantalising food ever.

'We'll see about that,' I says to myself. 'Here am I, starving hungry, with all that food going begging, I daresay. It's not right.'

'You stay here,' I says to the mice. I goes up to the door and gives it a bang. Some old porter opens it.

'Can't come in,' he says. 'You're trade.'

'Yeah, and my trade is punches.'

I give him a good left to the jaw and he goes over like a ninepin. He don't stir. Nice one, I say to myself. I pulls him into a corner behind the door and follows my nose to the smell.

And there it was. Out in the open. A table spread with more food than you've ever seen in your life. Cold meat, chicken, pies, pastries. And no-one about.

Well, whoever left that table unattended deserved what came to them. I made a right pig of myself. It was too good for humans. Rodent Rights should include food like that, so it should. For rats, that is, Rodent Rights not applying to mice. They'll just have to take their chances.

After a while, however, I'm absolutely stuffed. Couldn't have taken another bite to save my life. So I reckon I'm off to where the music's coming from, spy out the land, see what the opportunities are for a return visit some quiet night, know what I mean? And I want to know what that Cinders is up to.

So off I goes. And I spies Cinders, twirling round with some chinless wonder. She catches sight of me and as she passes her eyes narrow and she says, 'How dare you? Get out of here, you horrible rat!' and I says, 'Speak for yourself, you slag, or I'll tell Prince Charming here what you get up to down Oxpens Road Saturday nights.' So she shuts up – well, she has to, don't she?

Then I'm pulled into the dancing by a whole load of girls and, I tell you straight, I'm having a great time. I had more to drink than you would have thought possible and I snogged more than a few of the girls. I'd been a bit worried about what to do with my tail but I stuffed it down my britches so it wasn't visible. Anyhow, them girls is so drunk that they wouldn't notice if I had not just a tail but horns as well. Later on, that is, if I strike lucky with one of the girls. Know what I mean?

And so it goes on. And I'm wondering if I do score with one of the girls whether she really will be so pissed that she won't notice the tail and if she does notice how I'm going to explain it away when, all of a sudden, there's a great big smashing sound and there, careering right into the middle of the dance floor, is that coach and horses!

You should have heard the yelling and the screeching! All them blokes and them girls all throwing themselves about 'cos they was fearful of getting under the horses' hooves. And the horses, whinnying and rearing up, like something in a circus 'cept I could see they was really frightened, their eyes rolling back till you couldn't see nothing but the whites. And all frothing at the mouth. You'd never think that what they really was was little white mice.

I had to admit I was scared too. What with that and Cinders screeching at me, 'This is your fault, you stupid rat. Do something!' I was at a loss. I've been in the odd scrape from time to time and I've always been able to get out of it but this time, well, it was bleeding chaos.

I yells at Cinders, 'Your fault, you mean. Going off and leaving them nervous animals there.' And then she yells, 'You're the coachman. They're your responsibility.' And I yells, 'My responsibility, my backside. Get that daft old fairy godmother down here sharpish. She set this up, she can sort it out.' So Cinders gets out her mobile but how you call a fairy on a mobile, I wouldn't know.

Anyhow, so maybe it is my responsibility after all. Show those silly mice who's boss round here. So I sidles up to one of the lead horses, grabs the rein and pulls its head down. It stops careering about for a moment, just enough time for me to whisper in its ear that any moment now it was going to be midnight and we all know what happens at midnight and I've just seen a very large ginger tom lurking about in the bushes licking its chops. That brings them, all six of them, to their senses.

Then Fairy Godmother blows in, saying, 'Now then, now then, what's all this?' And Cinders starts carrying on fit to bust, but nothing to do with me or the mice. No, it's one of her slippers. She's lost it, silly little moo. So there's a right kerfuffle.

And then the clock starts to strike. Twelve o'clock, or I'm a Dutchman. 'Scarper,' I says to the mice, 'or you're food for the pussycat.' So they're off. And I am too. On my toes at the double. Shame about the fancy clothes but you can't win everything in life.

And what have I got? Well, that's the glass slipper. If Cinders wants to convince her prince that she's the belle of the Commem ball and not little Miss Nobody from Nowhere she'll have to do it some other way. I gave it to my dear old mum. She uses it for a vase and very nice it looks too.

THE TASTE OF MOONLIGHT

SYLVIA VETTA

The sitar strains of an evening raga and the scent of sizzling cumin seeds transported him home. The food served in the college dining hall seemed bland; he yearned for more aroma, more heat, more passion. When that need was strong, Rabindranath escaped here to the Moonlight Restaurant on the Cowley Road. How he wished he had learned to cook, but when did he get the opportunity? Jaswinder, their cook at home in Delhi, rarely needed help.

Moments when he ached for home would suddenly take him hostage. At a blink of an eye he could picture his sisters, Richa and Gia, as they knotted colourful rakhis around his wrist on full moon day in August, on the festival of Raksha Bandhan. The images were like video clips made with a shaky hand on the camera. He watched as they pretended to be damsels in distress calling, 'Help brother, help me I need you.'

He could feel the orange dust on his shirt as they chased him around the garden, pelting him with coloured powder. He could even see himself as he mock-protested, 'Is this the way to treat a hero?' and, adopting an austere voice of command, saying, 'Call for help as much as you like; this is one brother who won't fall for it.'

But of course, his sisters didn't need his help. Richa had set up her own design business in Delhi and Gia was studying to be an engineer. His parents had sent him to Oxford; they had political ambitions for him. As he sat at the plain pine table he thought what a dreadful disappointment he must be; he hadn't a political bone in his body.

His emotions seesawed as he waited for India to join him. He remembered their first date when he thought she was joking about her name. With perfect timing she stopped laughing at his incredulous face and explained how her parents went on the hippy trail in the sixties, following George Harrison and the rest of the Beatles to India.

'They met in an ashram in Rishikesh. I was conceived in India so they named me after your country.'

Seeing she had mixed feelings about their choice of name for her, Rabindranath had said, 'You're in good company; the Mountbattens called their daughter India.'

'Sure, and the Beckhams called their son Brooklyn, but parents forget it's their children who have to live with the consequences. How about *Rabindranath*? That's quite a mouthful.'

He was named after a politician married to his mother's best friend and confided, 'I hated it. At school, kids called me *bindi*, like the red mark Indian women paint on their foreheads. One clever clogs nicknamed me 'mad dog' when he discovered the word *rabid*. It was only at thirteen when I read the poetry of Rabindranath Tagore, that I started to own it, if you know what I mean.' India knew, but said she would call him Nat.

His thoughts were interrupted by her presence. He stood up and kissed her and she smiled with those intelligent and gentle eyes. Over the aloo tikki chaat, she leant towards him and whispered, 'Have you told them?'

'No not yet. What a coward I am. Dad says he's coming to England next month. You know he's a civil servant? Well, he's been promoted and moved to Defence. He's accompanying the minister; yes the one I'm named after – Rabindranath Mitra. They're going to an arms fair.'

Seeing India's reaction, he said, 'I feel the same; what is fair about weapons?'

She held his hand firmly. 'You'll tell him then?'

'That's the idea; take him for a walk on Port Meadow, show him the Arcadian scene and tell him his son wants to live in Arcady, that I've given up PPE for English Literature and have changed course without telling him. I expect he'll stop paying my fees; that's why I'm putting it off.'

'Don't be so pessimistic. Talk to him about Churchill who loved literature and Disraeli who wrote novels. Maybe he can meet Douglas Hurd; he was foreign secretary under John Major and also writes novels. Just don't tell him you won't ever go into politics.'

Suddenly Rabindranath had a voracious appetite. India always had an answer to every dilemma. She was so positive, a veritable life force, but he hadn't told his parents about his English girlfriend either. He knew he should before his father arrived but kept finding excuses.

With each passing week her presence in his life spread like roots, but essays, reading and tutorials seemed a good enough reason for putting things off. So when he arrived in London, his father was ignorant of all the changes his year in Oxford had made to his son's life. As the Oxford Express approached Marble Arch, Rabindranath twisted his fingers and bit his lip as he regretted his procrastination.

He walked with slow footsteps to the door of his father's room at the Dorchester but as he entered, Sunil Malhotra's face beamed with pride and he grasped his son in a warm bear hug. Rabindranath bent to touch his father's feet.

'It's good to see you son. Mummy-ji is sooo disappointed. She was so looking forward to seeing you but can't leave Nani-ji. You know how it is. Look at my baggage full of gifts from our female clan. While you open them I'll see to some urgent calls. Then what do you say to a walk in Hyde Park? I need a little respect after those sisters of yours; their latest craze is to talk to their poor father as if he were one of those filmi autocrats.'

Half an hour later they strolled around the Serpentine and Sunil began talking about a new book prize in India.

'Richa says it will be the Indian Booker. She went to Jaipur with that writer friend of hers.'

Rabindranath couldn't believe his good fortune and grasped the moment to tell his father about his change of course.

'If I can observe, read and then write, I'll have something to say. A degree in politics is OK but not necessary. What do you think? If I have insights into what motivates people, it could be more useful. Do you mind, Daddy-ji?'

'Mm, it's not what I would advise; you need some economics. What kind of a degree will you get? If you change course and don't get a first class honours – as I know you can, son – I won't be pleased.'

'Actually, Daddy-ji, working at a subject I love doesn't feel like work and I think I could be in with a chance of a First.'

Rabindranath couldn't believe how easy it had been. After all that unnecessary angst they parted as warmly as they had greeted. Sunil arranged to come to Oxford after the arms fair, and the negotiations were complete.

'The minister wants to see Oxford so you can show him around, introduce him to the Master. His lovely daughter is with him; Rama wants to do some shopping. It's too long since you last saw her.'

When he told India about his father's proposed visit to Oxford, she said, 'I'm a bit nervous; you'll have to give me some coaching on the etiquette.'

Seeing a flicker of guilt cross his face, she said, 'You have told him about me?' She could see the answer. 'Are you ashamed of me Nat?'

'Of course not, Indie. I'm gutted but I didn't know how to go about it. I'll book a table at the Moonlight to introduce him to my friends and you come along as one of them.'

India looked angry and hurt. 'Is that what I am to you, one of your friends? It's not what you said last time we made love.'

Shaken, Rabindranath stuttered, 'I'm h…hopeless, a novice at dating, no role models. My parents – all their generation – went through the system. Even now marriages are nearly always partly arranged, just more relaxed. Couples are introduced and then date to make sure of each other and can change their mind.'

India looked doubtful. 'You've become too important to me. When you graduate, you'll go back home and have an arranged marriage, won't you? Tell me now because I'd rather finish it and not be even more hurt.'

She turned her head, he realised, to wipe away a tear. Rabindranath's heart shuddered. The thought of her leaving him sent a physical pain racing through him. A sudden insistent desire made him unusually decisive.

'Indie, will you marry me? It won't be easy. I don't know what my family or your family will think or where we can live or how I'll make my living. I just know I want you with me.'

India felt God intended Rabindranath's huge honest brown eyes for a beautiful Jersey cow; in a man's face they seemed so unsettling. Her head felt unsure but how could anyone with a heart doubt the truth of that trusting look?

That evening ended in a resolution of a kind. They would marry but would give their prospective in-laws time to get to know them. They approached the first hurdle before they were even used to the idea themselves. The following Friday, their party of twelve would fill a side room at the Moonlight.

Rabindranath reflected on the day. His dad had been in jolly mood as they walked beside the Thames from Wolvercote. They stopped to watch the horses grazing on Port Meadow with the dreaming spires in the distance. Minister Mitra nudged his father and said something about, 'these young people'. Nodding towards his daughter Rama, he said, 'No miserable grey clouds in sight. Why don't you two carry on and finish the walk back to Oxford. Sunil-ji and I have things to discuss and there is someone I must see at All Souls. We'll see you both tonight. I can trust you to look after my daughter. She's much better company than two old men.'

Sunil looked none too happy with the *old*. Rabindranath's father, with his distinguished good looks, was often compared with Amitabh Bachchan, the Bollywood superstar. The minister was right about one thing; Rama was good company and she had been seeing a lot of his sister.

'You know Richa was in Vogue India last month. If she wasn't so charming with it, we'd hate her. How come one person can have everything - talent, good looks and a business brain also? Her clothes make women look sexy without looking silly. I've introduced all my friends. She helps them look attractive while being taken seriously. Has she told you about our plans?'

Rabindranath's look of ignorance brought a slight frown to Rama's smooth face. 'She talks about you, reads me your poetry, your short stories – everything – but she hasn't told you about us? I'll complain when I see her next. We're going into business together, *Richa and Rama*. Do you like the sound of it? Our aim is to expand, starting with branches in South Delhi and Mumbai but after that, maybe London.'

'Dr Mitra-ji, Dad, Rama, I'd like to introduce you to Paul and Rajiv. I think I told you about these two awesome mathematicians. Paul's just been offered a post doc and this is Jenny; Jenny's a nurse at the JR. We all met at a cricket match. Subhash is from Southall; he's keen to sell Richa's designs but he's never been to India. I've promised I'll bring him and introduce him to her next time I come home. Kwame is from Ghana, and this is my good friend India – no, you didn't mishear that – it really is her name.'

The dinner at the Moonlight felt formal but friendly, that is until the moment Jenny and Paul said they had some news.

'It's an invitation really. We've set a date for our wedding.' said Paul.

'It won't be till next year,' said Jenny. 'Paul's been offered a post at Imperial once he's finished his post doc and it'll be easy for me to find work anywhere as an intensive care nurse. But we want to get married in Exeter College Chapel before we move to London.'

Minister Mitra beamed and ordered champagne to toast the happy couple. As he put down his glass he looked from Rabindranath to Rama and from Rama to Rabindranath and said, 'It's about time you two started thinking about marriage. These romantic notions are very fine but in India, family matters. At your age, 24 going on 25, isn't it, your father and I had been husbands for three years.' He elbowed Sunil with a grin.

'Now it's your turn. Think of your families. It's a father's dream to raise a glass to his daughter and future son-in-law. Mind you, I prefer whisky to this fizzy French stuff.'

This was said in a mood of bonhomie but it didn't sound like a joke. India choked on her champagne, apologised and rushed out of the restaurant. Rabindranath ran after her.

'What do you mean you want to marry India? You stupid boy, you must have known that your mother and I intended you for Rama.'

'Actually daddy-ji, I didn't know; Rama's like a sister.'

'This is the thanks we get for trying to be modern, paying for your fine education. You stab your parents in the heart.'

Rabindranath sank into a chair feeling certain that the whole of the Randolph could hear his father shouting. Sunil glared at him.

'This English girl, you say you haven't even met her parents. So what do you know about her? It's an infatuation; you'll get over it.'

Tears appeared in his son's eyes. Rabindranath ground his teeth and clenched his hands until it felt as if his palms were bleeding but he said nothing.

Sunil threw up his arms and gestured towards the door. 'Suddenly I'm feeling my age. I'm going to bed. What a scene! What must Rama have thought? In the morning, see that you talk to her. Do you hear? Put things right with Rama.'

Unlike the previous day, the mood was dejected and tense as he and Rama headed for University Parks. As they neared the duck pond, he broke the silence, 'I don't really know what to say.'

'Let's sit down and you can start by telling me about her, about India,' said Rama. 'What does she do? How did you meet?'

'She's an actress, just starting out professionally. My first sight of her was as Roxanne in the OUDS production of Cyrano de Bergerac at the Playhouse. We met at a cocktail party in the rooftop restaurant at the Ashmolean. I was introduced to her just as the moonlight put stars in her hair. It was poetry.'

'So you're in love?'

His head bowed and his hands covering his face, he muttered a reply, 'Yes but what a mess I've made of everything. I've probably lost her and now I've hurt you too. What an idiot I am, an idiot in Oxford, where I came in search of wisdom.'

'You're not an idiot, Rabindranath and you haven't hurt me. You may even have done me a favour. You and I face the same problem. Our problem – yours and mine – is that we have to dare to be ourselves.'

Rabindranath looked up at her in disbelief. A passer-by seeing his mouth gaping wide, probably agreed with his self-assessment, but Rama ignored his look of stupefaction.

'I'm confused.'

'You're more than confused. You're blind to your own family.'

Seeing his look of abject misery, Rama sighed and said, 'I'm talking about your sister, Richa and... me. When I said we were partners, I didn't just mean *business* partners.' As the meaning of her words engulfed him, the tension drained from his face and he beamed at her and hugged her tight.

'Rama, you're a star,' he whispered, as he let her go. 'I have someone to see.'

He hurried off in the direction of Marston Road and India, overtaking the same passer-by. His look of disbelief once again questioned the young man's sanity because as he ran, Rabindranath laughed and his laughter illuminated his face.

'There the sun does not shine; neither do the moon and the stars; nor do these flashes of lightening. When he shines, all these shine: through his lustre all these are illumined.'

The Upanishads

THE BEAST OF SUMMERTOWN

BEN McSEOIN

It was almost hidden amongst an avalanche of rubbish bags and discarded Christmas trees, limping and stumbling from one pile to another.

When it saw Emily, it froze, in the same way a nocturnal animal does, then dived backwards and huddled against the ice-covered brick wall.

'Are you OK?' she called, conscious of her duty of care as a nurse.

It took a few moments before there was any response. By that time Emily's eyes had adjusted to the darkness and she began to make out its oddly shaped figure: human-like, but with bulky shoulders and a lumpen, misshapen back. It then turned and looked at her with its single bloodshot eye.

She took a step back and then another before beginning to walk briskly away. She was careful not to run; for all she knew, the Beast could have twelve metre claws capable of stretching out, capturing her and pulling her down into the depths of hell, from where it must have come.

But as she reached the end of the dark alleyway, and stepped into the dazzling light from the shopping parade, she thought she heard a voice call, 'Don't go.'

How on earth did she hear it? She was beside the busy Banbury Road on a Monday night; traffic was roaring up and down, normally drowning out any other sound.

But Emily did hear. Slowly she turned back and, at first, saw nothing. But as her eyes readjusted, she saw it, still slumped by the wall beside one of the dustbins. Cautiously she took a step closer.

Why, she wondered to herself. Why did she go back? Because it was lonely? Because it may have needed help? Emily didn't know.

'What's your name?' the voice asked as she slowly approached the figure in the darkness, being careful not to get too close, just in case.

Had Emily heard correctly? Had the... creature asked her name? Or had it asked something else? Had it even asked her anything at all?

'Comment tu t'appelle?' the voice then asked and, after a pause, 'Wie heisst du?'

Emily couldn't help but chuckle. 'It's Emily,' she said.

The creature grunted a few times, 'All these students… you never know any more.'

She smiled out of politeness and then asked, 'Are you hurt?'

'Just backache.'

'Can I… do anything to help you?' she asked.

'No thank you.'

Emily nodded in acknowledgement and then looked around, absorbing the area: the various bulky rubbish bags, the discarded clothes, furniture and other objects – probably unsellable donations to one of the charity shops - and the quiet rumble from a fan on the far wall blasting out hot air, easing Emily's tingling hands and feet. The creature likely gained comfort from it also.

'Do you live here?' she asked.

'Sort of,' the creature replied, 'When… no one's around. It's hard not to be seen these days.'

Emily nodded. What else could she do? She took a step backwards. The creature shuffled and Emily could see it was now nestled on top of one of the rubbish bags.

She opened her mouth to speak again but was interrupted by the sight of two gangly young men who came skulking out of Haddison College, and the sudden smell of cannabis filling the vicinity.

Had they seen or heard anything? She pretended to be adjusting her hair, running a finger through it, until they had disappeared into the darkness. Emily looked back but could see nothing but the same bulky black rubbish bags and green wheelie bins. The buzz of nearby traffic suddenly filled the alleyway.

A breath of winter sighed against her bare face, chilling her lips and eyelids and she shivered, searching for any form of life.

Where had it gone? Was it still there? Had it even been there to begin with?

Darren was standing in Blockbusters when she walked in, reading the synopsis on the back of one of the videos.

'Hi,' he smiled, kissing her on the cheek. 'Had a good swim? Are you OK? he added, looking at her more closely.'

'I'm fine,' she lied.

Why on earth didn't she tell him? He had a light attached to his bicycle; they could have gone back together and searched the dustbins thoroughly and then she could have proved to him that the Beast really did exist.

But, of course, when she finally did pluck up the courage to tell him, four days later, he didn't believe her at all.

'It was probably just some oddball. Oxford's full of them!'

'You didn't see!' Emily exclaimed. 'It had one bloodshot eye, a limp, a weird back and a deep, scary voice!'

They were sitting in the living room of their basement flat in Jericho, watching *Friends* on Channel 4; he looked away from the flickering TV screen and chuckled, 'Em, it was dark, wasn't it?'

'Pitch black.'

'Well then, the darkness can distort what we see. You ought to be careful going round there after dark anyway.'

'It wouldn't have hurt me,' Emily replied quietly, but Darren had already turned back to the television, too engrossed to hear anything else.

The following day while Darren was doing the weekly shop, she caught the bus to Summertown and went back to the same place, in daylight this time, but there was nothing. Just the same stack of bulky rubbish bags, wheelie bins and unwanted charity items.

She scanned the area thoroughly, catching the eye of an employee from one of the nearby shops who was standing against the brick wall, chewing on a cigarette. She felt herself blush, turned around, and walked briskly away.

That night when she got home, she drew a picture of the Beast, emphasizing its weird body and single red eye. She couldn't remember if it had horns, so she drew two pictures, one with horns and one without.

She planned to show it to Darren when he came home from football practice, but when he unlocked the front door and skulked in, bruised, muddy and in need of a hot shower, she quickly decided against it.

One week later, Emily went swimming again after her shift at the Warneford hospital, and took the same route as before so she could see the Beast.

But there was nothing.

She went back the following night, and the next night, and the night after that, until it became part of her evening routine. She began keeping a diary, logging in every single detail, any possible evidence that the Beast had ever been there. She even began rummaging through the actual site – scaring the odd urban fox and disturbing the occasional rat's nest in the process – to see if she could find it, lurking

115

deep amongst the rubbish. Maybe it was hiding; maybe it knew she was trying to find it.

But there was still nothing.

The months rolled by and as the longer, warmer days arrived, Emily continued to search; she soon got used to the stench.

One evening, when she came home from her nightly search, she found Darren sitting in the living room, his arms folded, the only light a small glimmer from the table lamp in the corner of the room.

'Who is he?' he asked, and then, when she didn't answer, he looked up at her. 'The guy you're seeing. You're coming home late. You didn't go swimming tonight; I know, because you didn't take your kit!'

Damn, Emily thought, her alibi had been blown.

'So who is he?' he snapped.

'It's not a he,' she replied 'It's an it.'

Darren looked at her, his eyes widening.

'I've been looking for the Beast,' Emily continued.

'The what?'

'The Beast. You know, I saw it amongst the rubbish bags. I know I saw it there and I'm determined to see it again.'

Darren's mouth and forehead crinkled in disbelief. 'My God, it's worse than I thought,' he muttered, getting up and walking out of the room.

'I'm going to find it,' she called after him. 'I know I will!'

The following evening, when she came home from work, ready to wash her uniform as she did every night – rummaging through rubbish bins was dirty work – she found Darren sitting at the kitchen table, his arms once again folded.

'You're back early,' she commented.

'I've booked you an appointment.'

'You've done what?!'

'With your GP, and I've told them why. You need a psychiatrist! They'll probably refer you to your own boss at the Warneford.'

'How dare you!'

'What you're doing is not normal,' he continued. 'But it's OK; there are people who can help you.'

She walloped him hard, wiping that patronising pseudo-reassuring grin off his smug face, and watched the remains of her once perfect relationship fall apart right before her very eyes.

He moved out soon after and it wasn't long before he'd shacked up with some rich, busty brunette in a penthouse flat in Belsyre Court.

Emily didn't care, even when the landlord forced her out of her own flat and she ended up taking refuge in a council flat on the outskirts of Blackbird Leys.

Emily didn't mind it there; the neighbours were nice enough and it wasn't too far from work, but trekking to North Oxford every night quickly became too much.

So she tended to spend a lot more time in Summertown, heading there straight from work, getting a bite to eat in one of the cafes or restaurants, until gradually each catering manager quietly informed her that 'people like her' were not welcome in their establishment.

Sometimes she stayed there all night. Initially, it was an accident; having missed the last bus back home, she chose to sleep at the Beast's home with a discarded mattress and blanket for comfort. And when she did survive the night, Emily realised how easy it was and chose to do it more often, twice, sometimes three times, a week.

Of course it caught the eye of others, staff and pupils at Ewert House, the various Summertown customers, and students from the various nearby schools and colleges. Some would stare, others would quickly look away upon seeing her sometimes lurking, sometimes sleeping, sometimes rummaging amongst the rubbish bags.

It was the teenagers who were less sympathetic.

'Oi, look! It's the Beast of Summertown!' one acne-scarred boy called to his equally ugly friends.

'I'm not a beast!' the dishevelled vagrant cried, as she rose from beneath the mountain of bags. 'I'm looking for a beast!'

But the teenagers just laughed and pulled out their mobile phones, all trying to snap photos or videos of her. Emily scuttled deeper into the mountain of rubbish bags making a mental note to remain hidden while people like that went past.

While sleeping in the Beast's home, she frequently overslept and, not having time to go home and have a shower, she went straight to the Warneford, where, after several warnings, she was dismissed for 'consistent lack of punctuality and presentation'.

As the years crept by Emily remained huddled in the same place where she'd first seen the Beast. She'd lost count of the number of times a policeman or social worker had tried to talk to her, tried to make her see sense, but she was determined to see the Beast again.

'It's been years now, Emily,' a police community support officer once sighed. 'I don't think the Beast is coming back. Why don't you just go home?'

'I can't give up,' Emily whimpered. 'If I give up now I'll have wasted all those years of my life.'

But then, one night as Emily sat there waiting, she saw someone, a shadow, coming towards her from the Ewert House car park. Was it the Beast? Had he come for her? After all these years?

It wasn't the Beast. It was just a man, a young man, but Emily still dived back behind the rubbish bags.

She watched him; he was tall, broad-shouldered and with light blonde hair – like her own hair used to be.

He stopped and looked in her direction and she quivered, her entire body filling with fear. She whimpered, trying to sound like one of the animals she'd often slept next to at night.

'Are you OK?' he called in a gentle voice.

Was he talking to her? There was no one else around; he must have been. Emily poked her head out slowly from behind the dustbins and looked at him. Could he see her? Obviously not, because he turned and started walking away towards the main road.

'Don't go,' Emily called.

He stopped and turned around.

He seemed nicer than all the other people, kinder and not condescending. But as he looked at her and cautiously began walking towards her, Emily felt her fear return. She scuttled back as far as she could until she was pressed up against the brick wall.

The man stopped when he reached the rubbish bags. What was he doing? Why was he staring at her? Could he see her?

'What's your name?' she asked him, if only to break the frightening silence.

He didn't answer; maybe his English wasn't very good. Oxford was filled with so many foreign tourists, students and academics these days.

'Comment tu t'appelle?' Emily asked, recalling her French A-Levels and, when he didn't answer, remembering her German O-Levels, 'Wie heisst du?'

The man chuckled, 'My name's Michael.'

So he was English after all. Emily grunted to herself and, not wanting to be rude, simply said, 'All these students… you never know any more.'

There was another awkward pause before Michael asked abruptly, 'Are you hurt?'

Not really, Emily thought to herself, apart from her aching shoulder blades, from the various uncomfortable things she'd forced herself to sleep on.

'Just backache,' she answered.

Emily stared up at him, wanting to see his face, to read his facial expression but it was far too dark.

'Can I… do anything to help you?' he asked.

Emily smiled, 'No thank you.'

She watched him as he looked at the Beast's home. Emily could tell what he was thinking before he asked her.

'Do you live here?'

'Sort of,' Emily answered, 'When… no one's around. It's hard not to be seen these days.'

Michael nodded. He looked as though he was about to speak again, but was interrupted by two teenage girls coming out of Haddison College.

They looked scary, Emily thought and, seeing one of them clutching a brightly lit mobile phone, she turned and hastily dived behind one of the wheelie bins.

She waited, petrified, until she was certain the girls had gone before creeping out to resume her conversation with the seemingly kind and concerned Michael.

But only after she had crawled out of her burrow and back into human sight, did she realise that Michael had already turned away and disappeared into the darkness.

ABOUT THE AUTHORS

Margaret Pelling took half a lifetime to remember that her first love was making up stories. Along the way there was research astrophysics, then the Civil Service, and then one day 'Yes, Minister' became 'Goodbye, Minister'. Her two published contemporary novels for adults are *A Diamond in the Sky* (Honno) and *Work For Four Hands* (Starborn Books). Another contemporary novel entitled *The Man Who Walks by the Sea* is almost finished, and a historical novel set during the aftermath of Trafalgar is at the research stage. More information at www.margaretpelling.co.uk.

John Kitchen was born in Cornwall, graduating in English and Education from London University. He taught in Cornwall, Worcestershire and Oxfordshire As a teacher he wrote plays and musicals for children, but retired from teaching in 2001 to write full time. He writes fiction for young people. His first book *Nicola's Ghost* (New Generation Press) won the New Generation Publishing Prize 2011 and *The Writer's Digest* Best Self Published Young Adult Novel 2011. His second book, *A Spectre in the Stones,* (Thames River Press) was published in May 2013. John's website address is www.johnkitchenauthor.com

Sheila Costello has had two children's novels published by Oxford University Press: *The Cats'-Eye Lighters* (1991) and *The Box That Joanne Found* (1995), both under the name Anne Lake. Apart from writing, her interests include dancing and music.

Liz Harris' debut novel, *The Road Back*, was published by Choc Lit in September 2012, and her romantic comedy, *Evie Undercover* (Choc Lit), is now out on Kindle. *A Bargain Struck*, set in Wyoming, 1887, is to be published in September 2013. She has written short stories for anthologies and her pocket novel, *A Dangerous Heart*, (DC Thomson, 2012), will be available in libraries in large print from May 2013. *The Road Back* and *Evie Undercover* were shortlisted for the Festival of Romance 2012 Awards, *The Road Back* for Best Historical Read and *Evie Undercover* for Best Romantic e-book. *The Road Back* has also been shortlisted for the Joan

Hessayon Prize. For more information or to contact Liz, please visit www.lizharrisauthor.com

Gina Claye has had children's poems published in anthologies by Scholastic and Oxford University Press and is currently working on a collection of children's poems. Her book *Don't Let Them Tell You How To Grieve* (OxPens) is used by Cruse Bereavement Care to help those who are grieving. She is editor of *Compassion*, the journal of The Compassionate Friends (an organisation of bereaved parents, siblings and grandparents supporting and caring for those similarly bereaved). She gives talks on bereavement to the Hospice Movement, CRUSE and other similar organizations and can be contacted at gina.claye@hotmail.com

Linora Lawrence has lived in Oxford for 30 years during which time she has worked at two colleges: St Hilda's and Trinity, the Bodleian Library and Oxford University Press. She writes for the *Oxford Times* and its monthly magazine *Limited Edition*, besides working on her own stories and a novel. She now realises that many of the people she has met in Oxford over the past years have unknowingly contributed to the tales she tells, for which she thanks them. She would also like to thank The Oxford Jewish Heritage Committee, and in particular their historian Ms Pam Manix, for generous help with research for her story in this book.

Chris Blount has been a contributor to all four anthologies. His story, *Platform 3*, is a parody on the classic wartime epic, *Brief Encounter*. He is currently writing a series of short stories for children with a sports theme from the point of view of the equipment, including *Gaspar the Goalpost* and *Susie the Swimming Cap*. Recently retired from 40 years as an investment manager, he is also Chairman of Oxford Homeless Pathways.

Heather Rosser has published articles in *Nursery World* and *The Midwives Chronicle* on childcare in Africa. She was also a journalist on the *Botswana Guardian*. Her children's book, *The Kombouka Ceremony,* was published by Macmillan. Since moving to Oxford she has written twenty Social Studies books for schools in Africa and the Caribbean. Heather's first novel, *African Twilight,* was shortlisted for the Constable Trophy and she is currently awaiting publication of her novel set in the First World War. You are welcome to visit her at www.heatherrosser.com

Rosie Orr lives in Oxford. Since winning the South Bank Show Poetry Competition she has had work published in several magazines and anthologies, including a *PEN* anthology, *The Virago Book of Love Poetry* and *WOW! 366!* Attica Books will be publishing her new rom-com *Romantic Variations (On an Italian Theme)* in spring 2013, which will be available in e-book and paperback.

Jane Stemp published two young adult novels, *Waterbound* and *Secret Songs*, with Hodder, while working as a librarian for the University of Oxford. She is now a rare books librarian for the Royal Naval Medical Service and, despite an 80-mile weekly commute, is still writing in what spare time she has. She can be contacted via her agent at David Higham Associates www.davidhigham.co.uk

Ray Peirson has written nine novels. All are now in e-book format and available from Kindle. They are mostly thrillers such as, *The Remorseful Assassin*, and the latest, *The Girl Who Was Murdered Twice*. He has also written two novels for older children/young adults called, *Slip Sliding Away*, and *Scorched Earth*.

Angela Cecil Reid, previously a teacher working with children with Dyslexia, now spends her days shepherding her rare-breed Cotswold sheep on her farm just outside Oxford, and writing. Her short story, *Arthur's Boy,* was commended in the Sid Chaplin Short Story Competition, while the opening chapters of her novel for Young Adults, *The Nile Cat*, reached the regional short list for Waterstones' Wow Factor Competition. She is currently working on a family biography to be published prior to the centenary of the outbreak of World War I. For more information, or to contact Angela, please visit www.angelacecilreid.com

Alison Hoblyn is a writer and artist. She has written magazine articles on gardens and their owners, and one novel, *The Scent of Water* (2005), which has a backdrop of Italian gardens. *Green Flowers* (Timber Press, 2009) is an illustrated handbook of garden plants celebrating their colour. Alison exhibits plant-inspired artwork, undertakes commissions and runs art workshops. She has lived in and enjoyed Oxfordshire and the city for more than 30 years.

Radmila May has lived intermittently in Oxford since 1987 but now lives in Chiswick in London although she comes back to the Writers' Group when she can. In addition to articles published in the literary and political journal *Contemporary Review* on subjects including Barbara Pym, the Yugoslav War Crimes Tribunal and a survey of crime fiction set in Oxford (*Murder Most Oxford*), she has been assisting in a new edition of her late husband Richard May's book, *Criminal Evidence.* Her contribution to this anthology arose out of an exercise set for an Oxford University Department of Continuing Education writing class.

Sylvia Vetta was chairman of The Thames Valley Antique Dealers Association when, in 1998, she began writing for *Oxfordshire Limited Edition.* Her profile features include Sharmi Chakrabarti, Colin Dexter, Roger Bannister, Peggy Seeger and Michael Rosen. Fifty profiles have been brought together in a book entitled *Oxford Castaways* with illustrations by Weimin He. She has written prolifically in other magazines about art and antiques and produced *Oxfordshire Rambles* for Kennington Overseas Aid. As chairman of the Friends of Kennington Library she has organised literary festivals and gala evenings. Contact Sylvia at: facebook.com/OxfordCastaways www.sylviavetta.co.uk

Ben McSeoin (Mc-Shown) has been writing – in one way or another – for as long as he can remember. *The Beast of Summertown* is based on a nightmare he had when he was three. He is currently in the process of self-publishing his first novel, a psychological drama, entitled *The Keyholder*. His interests include travelling, music, and foreign and art-house cinema.

The authors can be contacted at info@oxpens.co.uk. For more information visit the website at www.oxpens.co.uk and www.oxford-writers-group.co.uk.

The authors join together in thanking Chas Jones for his help and advice in the production of this fourth book in their Oxford short story series, and Gina Claye for her expertise, patience and diplomatic skills which she has brought to the role of editor whilst still finding time to be a contributor.

By the same writers

THE SIXPENNY DEBT AND OTHER OXFORD STORIES
First published in Great Britain 2006
Epub version (2011) ISBN 9781780185019
Kindle edition (2011) ISBN 9781780185002
Printed edition (2006) ISBN 9781780185149 (9781904623465)

THE LOST COLLEGE AND OTHER OXFORD STORIES
First published in Great Britain 2008
Epub edition (2011) ISBN 978178018503
Kindle edition (2011) ISBN 9781780185026
Printed edition ISBN 9781780185163 (9781904623120)

THE BODLEIAN MURDERS & OTHER OXFORD STORIES
First published in Great Britain 2010
Epub edition (2011) ISBN 9781780185057
Kindle edition (2011) ISBN 9781780185040
Printed edition (2010) ISBN 9781780185156 (9781904623243)

OxPens Publishing
www.oxpens.co.uk
www.oxford-writers-group.co.uk
Distributed through WritersPrintShop